CONNIVING WHISPERS IN THE MIDNIGHT SNOW

PRESTON'S STORY

~ PART 2 ~

CONNIVING WHISPERS IN THE MIDNIGHT SNOW

PRESTON'S STORY

~ PART 2 ~

YOLANDA RANDOLPH

Printed in the United States of America

Cover Design: Independent Designer

Editing, Formatting & Consulting:
LPW Editing & Consulting Services, LLC
The Editorial Midwife Publishing
www.litapward.com

First Printing, 2021

ISBN – 13: 9781-7343853-9-7

BOOKS BY YOLANDA

Twisted Tales of the Heart

Devious Deception Series

Wolf in Sheep's Clothing
Eyes of the Enemy
Vexed: Demise of a Sweetheart

Harriet High Series

Mysteries of Harriet High: "The Secret of Twila Anderson"
Twila's Dilemma: Field of Lies; Touchdown in Truth
Mommy's Girl

STAY CONNECTED WITH YOLANDA

Facebook- Yolanda Randolph Publications
Instagram- Yolanda Randolph
Twitter- YolandaRWrites
Website- www.yolandarandolph.com

GROUPS
Her Intuition Movement- Facebook Community
Pink Roses on Facebook and Instagram (a teen community)

PODCASTS
Her Intuition Movement- All Podcasting Platforms
ChiChat Podcast- Instagram, Facebook, YouTube
Her Intuition Live! - YouTube and Facebook

AWARD SHOW
Her Intuition Glow Awards

ACKNOWLEDGEMENT

First and foremost, I give all honor and praise to my heavenly Father, for seeing me through each and every obstacle that has come my way and for holding me at all times. I would be nothing without His grace and mercy.

To my children, thank you all for continuing to have my back. I love you forever and ever and a day! Lay, as you grow into a young woman, always know just how powerful your intuition is that God has placed in you. Follow it at all times and always remember that you are loved, you are worthy, and you matter. Make sure that others realize that too!

To all my family, godparents, friends, and my mentor, thank you all for standing with me in my journey. I love each and every one of you!

Finally, to my mom, Cynthia, and my grandmother, Pearl, my angels: I hope that I am making you proud from heaven.

CHAPTER 1

Preston glared at his son's mother and the person he held solely responsible for the unspeakable pain and anguish that threatened his sanity. "Bitch! If it wasn't for you, my son wouldn't be in there, having surgery right now!" Wiping the small beads of sweat off the top of his forehead, Preston leaned against the wall and placed both hands in his pockets.

"Baby, don't get yourself all—"

"Oh, you shut up! I don't even know…Why are you even here right now?!" Stephanie yelled at the tops of her lungs. Two of the nurses who sat at the nurses' station shook their heads in disbelief. Simultaneously, the other three watched in anticipation that Donald and Stephanie would go toe-to-toe again. Just as they've done when the frantic family followed the police officers to the Pediatric Surgical Intensive Care Unit. Preston's bright light and his everything, his son Jordan, was rushed to Sands Memorial for emergency surgery after shooting himself with his mother's gun.

"I'm here to support my man!" Donald yelled before rolling his eyes and placing his left hand on Preston's right shoulder. "Shit, instead of worrying about why I'm here, you need to be getting your story straight about how *your* son got to *your* gun in the first place."

"Don't worry 'bout me and my son. Bitch, if it wasn't for you, we wouldn't be here—"

"No!" Preston cried while snatching his hands out of his pockets, walking closer to Stephanie, and pointing his right index finger in her face. "You were the one who brought yo' ass over to my mother's house—"

"Yeah, ruining Thanksgiving! I was looking forward to some of yo' mama's greens too," Donald smirked and slowly shook his head for emphasis.

Looking over his shoulder, Preston used his eyes in an attempt to quiet Donald. Closing his eyes tight and slowly opening them, he focused his attention on the real reason why they were all at the hospital, his and Stephanie's son, Jordan. Nothing or no one else mattered to him at the moment. Not even his best friend, his lover, and his confidant, Donald, could bring his emotions down to a steadier level. Breathing deeply, he glanced at the ocean blue and the sunshine yellow wall that sat behind Stephanie. He

2

hoped that the vibrant colors would lighten his mood and his enormous dislike for Stephanie, and the lukewarm frustration he held for Donald.

"Listen, Stephanie," he started slowly. "I know—"

"My baby! Oh, God! Where is my baby?!"

All attention from the hospital's staff was immediately switched to the woman sporting a long blonde wig and slippers as she ran towards the family. The staff would tune back into the soap opera featuring Preston, Stephanie, and Donald shortly.

"Ma!" Stephanie yelled as she ran to greet her mother.

Preston slowly shook his head at Janet, a woman he disliked a smidgen more than he did her daughter, and rolled his eyes before glancing over at Donald. Donald stood tall, with his hands on his hips and a nasty stank face etched across his entire face.

"What happened?! Where is Jordan?!"

"He's in surgery, Mama. They said—"

"Surgery?! Stephanie, why is my grandson in surgery? I bet…" Glaring off in the near distance, she stormed towards Preston and Donald. "You did this!"

"Excuse me?" Preston squinted his eyes at a crying, frantic Janet.

"I said you! You did this, Preston!"

"No, your daughter did this!" Preston yelled back.

"Uh-huh, yeah, I bet it had something to do with that bitch you call a boyfriend over there!"

"Bitch?!" Donald stood up taller. "Now you wait just one damn minute! Who the hell you calling a bitch?!" Donald moved closer to Janet, readying himself for a verbal smack down.

"Mama, come on and sit down. Don't let that *thang* get your blood pressure up."

"Oh… see, y'all bitches asking for it."

"Bitches?!" Stephanie exclaimed. "Preston, you better get 'em. Before I whoop his ass like I did on the porch! You better get 'em."

Preston lowered his head as a few of the nurses snickered. *All of them can miss me with the bullshit,* he mumbled before grabbing Donald by the hand and moving him away from Stephanie and her mother.

"Hey! You folks are gonna have to take that outside!"

Preston sighed loudly at the sound of the hospital's security guard's deep baritone voice. Donald put his hands up in compliance while Stephanie and Janet continued their rant towards him.

"Now, ya'll! We can't have all that up in here."

"Alright!" Preston yelled loudly, startling everyone around him. "My son is in surgery, and ya'll out here acting like some damn fools!" To Preston's surprise, the crowd quieted, giving him a strong sense of seniority.

"Come on, Mama, let's go over there," Stephanie pointed towards the small opening that led to another one of the hospital's waiting rooms. "Before I have to smack somebody."

Preston turned all his attention on the security guard. Reading his name tag, he gently nodded his head. *Joe*, his mind recited before he spoke. "Joe, all that mess you saw, it won't happen again. My little boy is in there fighting for his life, and we are all just stressed out."

"Alright. I feel you, and I hope everything turns out alright," Joe said in a much lower tone than he had when he first walked over to the group.

"Thanks, man."

"Yeah! Thanks Joe!" Donald sarcastically called out.

Turning towards Donald, Preston frowned at the look of jealousy plastered all over his face. *Damn, you still acting stupid, huh? Just can't get away from the bullshit with him.* Moving closer to Joe, Preston extended his hand. "Thanks again, man." Preston nodded his head again before turning towards the small door with a replica of an ocean painted on it, giving a tight grip and firm handshake.

Thoughts of his son laughing and running towards him stung his brain, bringing a fresh set of warm tears to his eyes. *How could I let this shit happen? Then Mama, she...* stopping mid-thought, he thought of his mother, Annie, and her weak, frail frame as she was rushed away in a separate ambulance for symptoms of a heart attack. Seeing her grandson, with blood all over him, from a gunshot wound was too much for her. He pulled his phone out of his pocket, opened it, and searched for calls or texts from Madisyn. Although his mother was only a couple of blocks away from where he waited for the outcome of Jordan's surgery, he couldn't bring himself to leave the floor, even for a few minutes. *Madisyn's over there with her*, he assured himself for comfort measures. *I just can't leave my son. I need to be here when the doctors come out.* Turning his eyes, he landed on the glass that separated one waiting room from another. He rolled his eyes at the sight of Stephanie's hair and sucked his teeth at Janet's wig. *I hate both of them. I wish it were one of them, laying in the back, having surgery. Instead, it's my son, with doctors cutting into him.*

The blood popped into Preston's mind again, followed by the sight of his son's limp and lifeless body, and finally, the black pistol that caused all of it. Rage, yes, another bout of rage burned deep within the pits of Preston's gut, causing him to want to scream. Looking around, his eyes danced from Stephanie to Janet and then quickly landed on Donald, not sure of which of them he wanted to *off* first. *They are all getting on my nerves*! He whispered internally. Gazing over at Janet, he shook his head at her while she rolled her eyes at him. *Bitch*, he mumbled. Sighing, he slowly dragged himself to the small row of chairs that sat in front of him. Flopping down, he leaned his head back and focused his attention on the bright colors, and the drawings of small teddy bears holding balloons. Smiling, he noticed the hand-crafted art that stood tall above the teddy bears, all undoubtedly created by children. His mind immediately returned to his son and all the stick figures and tiny renditions of cars that Jordan loved to draw, just for him. Lowering his head, his eyes began to water, bringing the first set of full-fledged tears to escape. Something he'd been trying to avoid since he stepped foot into the hospital.

CHAPTER 2

L ay down, Mama. You shouldn't be moving around right now." Madisyn lightly pulled her mother's pillow, fluffed the ending closest to her, and readjusted it under her head.

"Maddie, I'm okay. I need to get up and get myself ready for church Sunday."

Madisyn flopped down on the hard hospital stretcher next to her mother. "Mama, you ain't going to church this Sunday. You are gonna be at home, resting in bed."

Annie looked away from Madisyn and stared off into the near distance. "Well, if I stay at home, it won't be to lay down in no bed. Have you heard anything from Preston? What about Jordan?"

The million-dollar question... If I tell her he's in surgery, she'll worry and get her pressure all up again. If I lie, then I'll be so wrong for—

The door flung open, grabbing both Madisyn's and Annie's attention.

"Ma!"

Annie cleared her throat before smoothing her right hand over the top of her salt and pepper-colored hair. "Leon, hey, son."

Madisyn stood up and hugged her brother before giving a quick wave to his wife. "Hey, Leon."

"Wassup, Maddie."

Madisyn moved over to the side of Annie's bed and watched as Leon hugged and kissed their mother.

"How you doin', Ma?" Leon asked while surveying the tubes and the machines that were attached to his mother. "You alright?"

"Oh, I'm fine, baby."

"Hey, Deborah."

"Hi, Ms. Annie. How are you feeling? You alright?"

"Oh, yes! Look here… y'all quit that worrying 'bout me. I'm okay. What about Deb? I ain't heard nobody mention her since those police came to the house and dragged her off to jail. Did y'all get her out?"

Chimes and bells rang above Annie's head, causing the family to pause.

"Ma?"

"Oh Leon, I'm alright. I promise. Those things been going off since I got in here, and bells or something or other, on this thing they call a bed, been making all kinds of noises. Now, y'all better start doing some talkin'. I wanna know what's going on with my family."

Madisyn sighed internally and flopped down in the chair across from Annie.

"What is going on with Jordan? How is he doing? What about Preston? And…" Annie clutched her chest as coughs interrupted her questions. She sat up in bed, trying her hardest to catch her breath.

"Mama, you—"

Annie put her hand up, immediately silencing Madisyn. Madisyn glanced over at Deborah and shook her head. Deborah smiled uncomfortably while repositioning herself against the wall.

"Now, I want to know what is happening with my family. My grandson is going through, my niece is up in some jail, and y'all won't tell me nothing. I want y'all to—"

"Ms. Annie, try to relax."

"Deborah, I want to know what in the world is going on!"

"Okay… Yes, ma'am. I will go and see what's going on with Jordan, Preston, and Deb. But you gotta promise me that you'll relax," Deborah smiled warmly, hoping that her smile would relax her mother-in-law.

The entrance opened, bringing stillness to the room.

"Ms. Annie, how are you doing?"

All eyes turned to Devin, Annie's nurse.

"Hey, young man, I'm doing alright. Ready to go on home. I gotta get myself ready for church come Sunday."

Devin chuckled while pushing buttons on the machine that sat closest to Annie's bed. "Well, you got to get an ECHO, and then we will see after that."

"ECHO?" Annie repeated.

"Just a fancy way of saying a picture or a scan of your heart," Devin smiled and patted Annie on her right shoulder. "Dr. McCloud wants to make sure you are healthy enough to go home."

"So, did she have a heart attack?" Leon asked.

Devin clicked his pen in writing position. "No, we didn't find evidence of one; it looks like she had a spasm. Which can sometimes seem like a heart attack."

"A spasm?" Leon frowned.

"Yes, one of her coronary arteries," Devin said as he wrote some notes down on the small piece of paper he was carrying.

"Devin, that's my son, Leon, and his wife, Deborah."

"Hi," Devin extended his hand to Leon and then to Deborah. "Nice to meet you both."

"Hi," Deborah spoke.

Leon nodded his head before placing his eyes on the bag of liquid Devin held in his hand. Following Leon's eyes, Devin smiled and lifted the bag so Leon could get a better look. "It's just some fluids. She was dehydrated when she came in so, this'll fix all that."

"Oh," Leon responded in a voice that wasn't his own.

All eyes remained on Devin as he stuffed the piece of paper and pen in his pocket and removed an empty bag from off the machine pole before replacing it with the new one. The family watched while Devin tapped a few buttons on the machine, opened a compartment, slammed it shut, and clicked one final button that sat above all the rest.

Okay, Ms. Annie, hit your call bell if you need anything. Is it on your bed?

Annie patted the side of her bed before sitting up.

"Nah, Ma, just lay down. We'll find it," Leon called out before walking closer to his mother.

"Here it is," Devin said as he pulled the medium-sized box from underneath the side of the bed and clipped the small silver clip to Annie's blanket.

"Thanks, man."

"No problem."

Annie smiled while patting Devin's hand. "Thank you, son."

"Sure, no problem. Get some rest. We'll hopefully get you down to get your ECHO soon." Devin smiled at the family before pulling the paper and pen out and scribbling notes on it; he dropped it back down into his lab coat's pocket. Hitting the sanitizer pump, he smiled again before walking out the door. Annie loudly cleared her throat and looked around at her family, focusing more on Deborah.

"Deborah—"

"Yes, ma'am, going now."

Madisyn nodded. Annie sighed, no doubt a sigh of relief that someone was finally listening to her and checking on her family.

"Baby, I'll leave the girls at Mama's; they can go and see the baby next week instead of tonight."

"How is my Lil stinka doing?" Madisyn shifted in her seat and tilted her head towards Deborah.

"He's good. The doctor said he might get to go home sometime in the next few weeks. Maybe next week if he continues to pass his oxygen trials."

"Praise God!" Annie cheered. "I told y'all that baby was strong. Just because he was born early doesn't mean he won't be alright."

Deborah chuckled, "That's right. Okay, let me head over to the children's hospital and see if Jordan's out—"

"Mama, do you want something to drink?" Madisyn said as she flashed a slow blink at Deborah. Turning to

Annie, she pursed her lips. "You haven't had anything to drink in a while. Let me go and see if they can get you something."

"Alright. I am a little thirsty and hungry too. I wouldn't mind having something from Dominick's right about now. Some good ole crab cakes and a few of their cheddar biscuits would do me just fine right about now.

"Deborah, come on, girl."

Deborah winked her left eye at Madisyn before turning to the sanitizer station and lathering a healthy amount onto her hands.

"Alright, Ms. Annie, I'll be back."

"Leon, try to keep your mama calm."

"Yeah, I'll try," Leon inhaled while placing his eyes on Annie. "She just looks so—"

"Just talk to her," Deborah said as she rubbed her husband's back. "Talk to her about the baby or something. Something cheerful."

"Yeah," Madisyn jumped in. "Won't you talk to her 'bout going to church with her sometimes? That'll get her in good spirits. A good miracle always gets people in a happy mood."

"Shut up, Maddie," Leon laughed.

Madisyn licked her tongue out at her brother and opened the door to walk out.

"Y'all done started that toying 'round," Annie laughed.

Both Madisyn and Deborah laughed aloud, happy that Annie was cheering up a bit.

"I'll be back," Deborah said before following Madisyn out the door and into the brightly lit and boisterous hallway. Keeping a reassuring smile on her face, Deborah slowly closed the door before she let into Madisyn.

"Girl! Your mama don't know—?"

"Shhh…Why you so loud?!" Looking around, Deborah waited for a group of visitors to pass before she spoke further. Clearing her throat, she shook her head at Madisyn. "What? I didn't think I should be worrying her with Jordan being in surgery and all that. She don't need to hear that right now."

"Yeah, but Maddie, you know she's gonna find out, and when she does…" Deborah stopped and shook her head. "Girl, let me go and see what's going on with Deb. Well, I'll go over to the hospital and check on Jordan and Preston first before I go over to the jail. Preston hasn't tried to call you?"

"Nope," Madisyn leaned against the wall and folded her arms.

"He might've tried. The reception is so bad in here; maybe he tried and couldn't get through."

"Yeah… maybe."

"I'll go over there, check everything out."

"Thanks, girl," Madisyn replied and chuckled. "Deb put dem paws on that ole bitch, though."

Deborah laughed. "Girl, that was an ass-whoopin' waiting to happen. Your cousin was not playing with her. I'm glad Deb beat her down. I mean, who goes to somebody's house on Thanksgiving and starts a bunch of mess?"

"That bitch Stephanie, that's who!" Madisyn laughed. "And I thought I was crazy. I've done a lot of things over the years, but the one thing I've never done was go over Chad's house and start some shit with his family."

Deborah laughed before throwing Madisyn an enormous side-eye. "Chile, please! You ain't never started no stuff with Chad, but you damn sure caused your share of shit with them other dudes."

"Them lames don't count." Madisyn rolled her eyes, waved her left hand, and placed the other on her hip. "Shoot, they better be glad I didn't do more than just slash a couple of tires and bust out a few windows."

"Girl…" Deborah laughed. "Let me go."

"Thanks, sis-in-law, and call me when you get over to the hospital. If it is the reception messing up, call the main desk, and ask for Mama's room. Her nurse said he would bring a phone in there for us."

"Okay, well, let me go ahead and go. I think it's supposed to snow later tonight, and you already know. I ain't trying to be all up in it."

"I feel you."

Deborah nodded her head, pushed another generous helping of sanitizer in her hands, and walked away.

Humph, her, and her sanitizer, Madisyn mumbled before turning to go back into her mother's room.

The clicking of the door alerted Preston, bringing his head up and giving his full attention to whoever was coming out from behind it. Preston saw the tail of the white lab coat first, followed by the end of the multi-colored, polka dot tie that Jordan's doctor was infamous for wearing. Standing, he walked closer to the door, just as the doctor emerged completely from behind it.

"Mr. Dixon?"

Preston nodded his head as he moved closer to the doctor. "Dr. Haven! How's my—"

"He's stable," Dr. Haven nodded. "We have a long recovery ahead of us, but we are hopeful that he'll pull through."

Looking up in the air, Preston lifted his hands in awe and praise to God. "Thank You, Father," he muttered. The doctor's remaining update was all a blur as all Preston waited to hear was already said. Glancing back over his shoulder, he looked for Donald, but Donald was nowhere around to his surprise. Looking back at the doctor, he smiled. "Thank you so much, Doctor."

You're very welcome.

"I need to see him."

"Certainly, just as soon as we get him to his room and comfortable, we'll bring you back."

Preston's temperature began to rise, and his stomach matched with the flips that were roaring deep within. "Where is he?"

"He's still in recovery. We're watching his—"

"Nah, Doc, come on now. I want to see my son. I don't want to wait until he's in a room. I want to see him right now." Preston put his head down and breathed in a strong cleansing breath. "I-I'm sorry, Doctor. I just—"

"It's okay, Mr. Dixon. I'm a father myself, and I understand."

Preston looked up at the doctor, careful not to allow the tear to fall that hung for dear life onto the beginning tips of his lower eyelashes.

"Doctor!"

Preston rolled his eyes at the sound of Stephanie's voice.

"Is my son alright? Did the surgery go—"

"Yes, we removed the bullet from his abdominal wall. He's an incredibly lucky little—"

"His abdominal wall?"

Preston glared at Stephanie. "His stomach, you stupid—"

"Hey!" Janet hissed. "Don't start with your mess."

Thinking of his promise to the security guard, Preston lifted his hands and moved closer to the doctor.

Rolling her eyes and balling both fists, Janet turned to her daughter before focusing all her attention on the doctor. "What about my grandson?!"

"Well, he's stable," Dr. Haven answered. Looking over at Preston, he waited for a sign that he should speak further. Preston nodded his head, giving him permission to move further with the discussion.

"Wait! Why are you looking at *him* and waiting for *him* to give *us* permission? He's my son too!"

"Yep, says the mother who left a gun in the presence of her *son*! You're negligent!" Preston yelled. Catching the nurses' snickers and chuckles as they watched the show of his and Stephanie's drama, Preston lifted his hands. "I don't have time for this. Jordan is hurt, and you sittin' here asking the man who helped him dumb-ass questions."

"Doc, I need to see my son. Can you please take me to him?"

"Well," Dr. Haven dropped his head slightly. "Just one person at this time. He's still in recovery."

"Well, I'm going first!" Stephanie lifted her left hand towards Preston.

Preston angrily chuckled before shaking his head and walking away.

CHAPTER 3

W hat is the matter with you?! You going over to his mama's house was never a part of the plan!" Donald hissed. As he looked around the empty parking lot, his eyes fell on the small shadow that the light, hanging high above them, cast over the area.

"Uh, you never said not to go over there. I didn't know that little boy was in the car."

"Yeah! But didn't you…" Donald sighed loudly as Preston's tensed face and red, tear-stained eyes burned furiously in his mind. Breathing in deeply, he squinted his eyes before he continued. Looking back over at the shadow, he focused his attention on the tiny snowflakes that began to fall.

"Didn't I what… *Dad?*"

"I'm not your… Look, I don't have all night to spend here with you, Heather." Donald quipped back.

"Well, I don't have all night either. So, come on and pay me my money so I can go handle my business."

"What?! Are you kidding me?! I'm not paying—"

"Yeah! The snow starting early this year."

Donald leaned back against the wall as two men briskly walked by.

"Yeah, that bus better not be late. Boss Man worked the hell out of us today, and I'm ready to go home and lay it down for the night," the man with a hard, yellow construction hat roared.

"Hell yeah!" his friend laughed.

Donald kept his eyes on the men until they became silhouettes under the light's shine. Moving his eyes from one vision to the next, he refocused his attention on Heather. Becoming aggravated and a bit ashamed, he studied her. *How did I allow myself to walk away from a girl I used to call my own? How could I disappoint her father like this?* A female version of Chris stared back at him with a hint of sadness and despair, gripping her eyes. His mind reverted back to the happy days. Days when he and Chris were in love and in deep planning mode of their future. Until the unthinkable happened.

"Let me go! I don't have time for you and your staring. I hated it back then, and I still hate it now."

Donald brought his mind back to the task at hand and his newest reality. The girl in front of him, the girl he once called his stepdaughter, was now responsible for shooting his stepson. "What a mess," he muttered while stuffing his left hand in his pocket.

"Come on, Don. Give me my money so I can go on with my life. Me and my daughter got shit to do!"

"What?" *Your daughter?*

"Look, man, just give me my money." Forcefully pushing out her right hand, she eyed Donald intently. "I want my money. Now, I didn't mean to shoot the little boy, but he was there, so he got it. It's that simple."

Anger and rage forced their way into Donald's mind. "I told you to shoot and *kill* that bitch, not her child! You messed it all up, and now…" The image of Preston's distressed face reemerged, causing a small tear to form within the deepest folds of Donald's tear ducts. *I never meant for any of this to happen*, he whispered. "None of this. Now a little five-year-old boy is laying in the hospital, hurting because you couldn't get it right." Shaking his head, he lightly dusted off some of the snow that had fallen on his hat. "I gotta go. You messed up, so you aren't entitled to the money that we agreed on. Five thousand dollars would've been good for you. Seeing that you still ain't got shit." Allowing the anger to overpower him, a defense mechanism he possessed during his early days of coming out to his family about his sexuality, he continued with the manufactured rant. "I can look at you and tell that you are in desperate need of money. Not only to take care of you, but now you got a lil bastard child to take care of."

Heather gasped and pursed her lips. "Bastard?!"

The look of surprise excited Donald, hyping him up to continue. "Yeah, I bet you would like the money, but I just ain't gonna give you something that you don't deserve. You brought the gun, you shot, but you failed at handling the task, so for that, you gets nothing!" Taking one final glance at Heather, he removed his hand out of his pocket and casually walked away.

Where the hell is Don?! Preston screamed internally. Sitting in the chair, he looked towards the door, thinking of his son lying in one of the beds behind it. Leaning his head back against the wall, visions of Stephanie and her mother

28

forced their way at the forefront of his thoughts. The feel of hatred grabbed his heart and stung his brain as he allowed them to go in to see Jordan first, without a fight. "I hate them," he said aloud. A bit too loudly as one of the drama-seeking nurses looked over at him. *They so damn nosy. Been looking over here at me all night.* Slightly shaking his head, he repositioned himself in the chair. Closing his eyes in hopes of finding something other than Stephanie, Janet, the disappearance of Donald, or his son's injured body, he relaxed his muscles and forced it. Thoughts of his mother came to mind, easing him a bit. Until her memory too turned to the negative side with the sight of her clutching her chest in pain. Popping his eyes back open, he sighed and fixed his eyes on nothing in particular.

"Preston."

Preston looked over at the sound of familiarity calling his name. "Deborah!" Standing, he rushed over to his sister-in-law, grateful that a line of comfort was finally in his presence.

"Hey, how you holding up? How's Jordan?"

"Well, he's out of surgery. But he's… Damn!" he gawked as the drama squad watched in anticipation of more scenes of Preston's dramatic life. No doubt hoping that

Deborah was bringing more tea for each of them to sip. "Come on, Deb," Preston gently pulled Deborah's hand. "Let's go over there," he said before rolling his eyes at the nurse with the purple Mohawk. He frowned as the nurse smacked her lips and mumbled something under her breath.

Deborah chuckled, "Don't be letting them girls get the best of you, Bro. They sit here all day; I'm sure they need something to make the time go by."

"Yeah, whateva. How's Mama?"

"She's doing good. Sitting up talking and wishing you were there. Oh, and most of all, she ready to get up out of that bed."

"Yep, I bet," Preston smirked. "Yeah, I tried calling, but—"

"No reception, I know. That's why I'm here. I came to update you and to check on you and Jordan."

"Right," Preston said as he watched a new family rally around the space he had been holding since he got there. A woman looking just as distraught and worn down as he did flop down in the seat where he was sitting. Looking back at the waiting room where Stephanie and her mother previously sat, he motioned for Deborah to follow him as he searched for a vacant space.

Yeah! A group of animated characters sang out from the TV that sat high in the corner. *Let's go this way*! They called out as a happy, child-engaging tune burst through the TV and into the waiting room. Walking over to a space in the corner, directly across from the TV, Preston sat down. He waited as Deborah fiddled with her phone. He looked out in the open hall, making sure the door which led to Jordan's bed was still in clear view.

"That was Maddie; I told her I would text her to let her know when I got here. I hope it goes through. The reception at the hospital is so bad. We're gonna try to get a phone in Mama's room so you can talk to her."

Preston nodded his head. "Oh, so, how's my mama really doing? You know how she likes to say she's good and really not be doing so well."

"Nah, she's good. You know I would tell you if I knew she wasn't." Deborah sat down next to Preston. "She didn't have a heart attack, they don't think. Just some type of spasm or something. Her doctors are gonna run some tests, though, just to be sure."

"Thank God," Preston exhaled.

"Yeah, Mama Annie is a tough ole woman. Some lil spasm ain't gonna take her out."

Preston chuckled. "Right, thank you for coming. I really do appreciate you."

"Yep, you know I got yo' back. We family, and that's what family do."

"Yeah." Looking over at the door, he sighed and put his head down. "I just wish Stephanie would get her ass out of there so I can go back. I haven't seen my son since we got here."

"That bitch. She the reason why he's here."

"Right!" Preston lifted his head.

"Her ass should be in jail instead of taking up the time. Did you tell them that she is the one who left a gun around? That she was the one who left a gun in the car... with her child?"

"Nah," Preston shook his head. "I need to..." Preston's reply drifted off at the sound of muffled cries. Looking towards the sound, he stood up as Stephanie and

Janet emerged from the area he wanted and needed to get to the most.

"Finally," Preston murmured. *"*Come on, Deborah. Let's go."

"Nah, you go. I'll wait out here for you. You go ahead and see Jordan, and I'll—"

"No! I can't go in there by myself. He can only have one person in there at a time, but you can wait by the door for me, and then you can—"

"Preston…Yes, you can." Deborah stood up. "He's your baby. You should go and let him know you are here, here for him."

Stephanie quickly whipped by, being sure to flash Preston and Deborah one final stank eye before she made her way to the visitors' elevators.

"Oh, that bitch! You think she'll stay up here? At least 'til the police come and get her crazy as—"

"Oh no, you don't! I will not have you talkin' bout my daughter that way."

Deborah turned towards the harsh voice and menacing stance of Janet, readying herself for the challenge.

"I'll talk about that crazy bitch anytime I want!" Surveying Janet from the top of her lightly matted blonde wig to the bottom of her pink slippers, she smacked her hands on her hips and waited for Janet to respond.

Looking over at Preston and then back at Deborah, Janet shook her head and stormed off, surprising everyone involved.

"Huh, that's shocking. The bitch ain't got nothing to say."

Preston placed his hand on Deborah's shoulder. "I'm glad she walked away. I don't want to have to deal with you and my cousin sitting in jail together. Ya'll already got the same name; I don't want y'all sitting up there together. That's bad luck," he chuckled. "I wonder if somebody went up there yet to bail her out."

"Nah, not yet, but I'm getting ready to head down there. I wanted to check on you first, though."

Preston looked over towards the door. The cheerful fish that were painted on it appeared to look more like flesh-eating, hungry piranhas than the hand-crafted art of happy, cheerful children. His nerves were getting the best of him, and a prolonged conversation with his sister-in-law seemed to help subdue some of his feelings. *Where the hell is Donald?*

"Aye, where is Don?"

She read my mind. "Uh, I don't know. He was here one minute and gone the next."

"Oh… well, let me go. You go on in there and see your baby. Give him a big kiss for me."

Thoughts of what he may or may not see intimidated him. Not sure what to expect, he put his head down and nodded.

"Come on, bro, pull yourself together."

Slowly bringing his head back up, he lightly tugged on Deborah's hand. Looking over at what was now mentally known to him as the door of mystery, uncertainty, and doom, he sighed. "Can you just come—"

"No, you got this." Deborah looked over at the large window that sat at the end of the hall. The small sheds of snow that were falling previously were now at full capacity. "Look, it's snowing hard now. I need to go ahead and get over to the jail to see about Deb. Then I have to go and check on the kids. Oh, and before I go, I need to run downstairs to the NICU while I'm here. My breasts are about to pop with—"

"Um, okay… I got it."

Deborah gingerly smiled at Preston. "I'll be back to check on you in a little while. You don't have any idea where Donald is right now? I would think he would be here, with you."

Preston shook his head slowly and then looked over at the window. "Don't know," he responded while shrugging his shoulders.

"Humph. Well, I'll check on you in a lil while. Love you."

"I love you too, Sis, and thanks for everything."

"Yep," Deborah quipped before slipping her coat on and rushing towards the elevator.

Watching Deborah until she was out of his sight, Preston folded his arms and focused his attention on the snowfall. What awaited him scared him beyond belief, causing him to stall. Yes, he wanted to see his son and make sure he knew his daddy was there and by his side, but the fear overpowered him. The familiar feeling of defeat grabbed him, the same way it did when his father lay dying of cancer at the same hospital his mother was now lying in. Looking up towards the ceiling, a pinch of a glimmer spread across his eyes at the array of bright colors that lined it.

"Mr. Dixon?"

Startled, Preston steadied his head back at eye level, acknowledging Dr. Haven. A look of sorrow displayed on the doctor's face, bringing a look of bewilderment onto Preston's.

"Doctor…" Preston started.

"Mr. Dixon, Jordan has slipped into a coma. We're doing everything…."

Preston's ears suddenly began to burn; a loud ringing and popping sound followed. Dr. Haven's face became a blur, and so did everything else around him.

"He's… medicated…." Preston heard the doctor say as his ears bounced in and out of their functions. "Stabilized…" another portion of the chat wiggled its way into Preston's comprehension.

"Mr. Dixon?"

The heaviness slowly subsided, allowing Preston's senses to refocus and become clearer.

"Can I get you some water?"

Clearing his throat, Preston shook his head. "No," he whispered. The word "coma" seared deep into his mind. "Coma?"

Dr. Haven nodded his head. "I know this is a difficult time for you, and I just want you to know that we are doing everything we can."

Preston nodded his head.

"I'll be sure to keep you and your wife—"

"What?" Preston mumbled. "My wife? Nah, that bitch ain't my wife!"

"I see." Dr. Haven cleared his throat. "Well, we'll keep you… and Jordan's mother informed sir," the doctor replied before turning and walking away.

Beginning to feel faint, Preston leaned his head back against the wall. Hoping that it was strong enough to steady him, to keep him from falling.

CHAPTER 4

Breathing deeply, Donald kicked off his snow-covered boots and threw his keys onto the couch before walking into the kitchen. Gaining comfort from the small wall clock that ticked above, he inhaled deeply and then exhaled. *What is wrong with that girl?! I ask her to do one thing, and she…* Leaning against the counter, he placed his hands on his head and shook lightly. *I should've known better.* "A drink. Yeah… all I need is a… wait! What am I talkin' bout?" He chuckled. "We ain't got no drinks here. Pres… Damn!" He huffed. Looking up at the clock, he frowned before stuffing his hands in his pocket and pulling out his phone. "10:25… I should be at the hospital instead of being here. Maybe I should—"

"Should've checked on him."

Dropping his phone, Donald swiftly turned, finding a larger, more intense version of the Dixon family males, Leon.

"Uh, what are you doing—?"

"Lookin' for you. I asked about you and heard that you left the hospital; without saying a word to anybody. Why are you here?"

"Um," Donald began. *I really wish we kept drinks in the house.* "I just came home to get Preston something to eat and… *changing clothes… yeah.* And some changing clothes," he repeated the chant that his mind was pushing.

"Right," Leon said dryly.

Retrieving his phone, Donald tapped his code in and immediately went to his missed call log. There was nothing. Looking over at Leon, he swallowed the gulp of air, holding his mouth hostage before moving over to his text messages. He was met with the same response. "Maybe I should try to call him. Is he alright?"

Leon pulled a chair out from underneath the table and slowly sat down. "You tell me. You're his man; you should know If he's alright."

Donald tilted his head and sat his phone on the counter.

"So… we gonna sit here and play stupid all night?"

"Huh?"

"Huh?" Leon mocked. "What was all that whispering and mumbling I heard when you first walked in?"

"Whispering? Mumbling?"

"Yo, man, stop trippin'." Repositioning himself in his seat and massaging his left shoulder, Leon closed his eyes. "I heard you. You was mumbling or some shit about asking somebody something and—"

"Oh," Donald nervously giggled. "I was just talking about the buses. You know how the buses out here can be when it starts snowing. They be actin' all scared of the snow when we first get it."

"Snow."

"Yeah, you know how it is."

"Yep, I do," Leon nodded his head. Standing, Leon snickered before making his way out of the kitchen and into the living room. Donald anxiously waited to hear the front door open and close. A second later, the sound he'd wished for interrupted the silence, bringing his mind, body, and spirit to a huge wallop of relief.

"How the hell did he get in here? I know I didn't… Humph… Preston," he seethed. "I told him not to be giving his people keys to our house! My house!" he quipped as he stormed through the kitchen and into the living room. "Shit, I never heard a car start." Diminishing his roar to the size of a cat's purr, he quickly walked over to the window. Peeping out, he found his yard and the immediate surroundings empty. *His big ass gone*, he muttered as he pulled the curtain back a bit further, making sure to survey all of his yard. Thin layers of snow replaced the manicured, vibrant grass and the decorated flowers planted in it along the walkway. Moving over to the adjacent window, his eyes fell on the partially covered boot prints, signifying that Leon had, in fact, left. "In my damn house!" He yelled. Now that his unexpected guest was gone, he felt free to yell as loud as he wanted.

"Not now!" Heather screeched. "I'm trying to hurry up, but I can't if you don't shut up!" She squinted her eyes tight until her three-year daughter, Ashanti, ran away. *Little bitch*, she mumbled under her breath as she grabbed the small bag of rice and poured the remainder of it into the small silver pot of boiling water. The beginning stages of one of her many migraines began to take root, further infuriating her. Laughter from happy children, interacting with their favorite life-sized, animated teddy bear named Scruff, exploded from the TV screen in the living room. Instead of being a welcomed distraction for kids, it just intensified Heather's headache. "That damn bear," she huffed as she grabbed a spoon and began stirring the rice. "Somebody needs to tell that child that the damn thing ain't real."

"Aye! Where y'all at?"

"Oh damn, now her ass is here. I just can't get a fuckin' break."

"Grandmaaaaa!" Ashanti squealed.

"Hey, baby!"

Heather rolled her eyes, snatched the lone pot cover from the empty dishrack, and slammed it on top of the pot.

"Uh oh, looks like your mommy is in one of her moods, Ashanti." Looking back up at Heather, Brooke smile politely and said, Hey, girl."

"Hey," Heather offered a sour reply.

"Oh, so you are in one of your moods."

"Nope, just cooking."

Sitting her purse on the counter, Brooke walked over to her daughter and wrapped her arms around her.

"Get off me!" Heather spat. "Don't put your damn hands on me." Heather's eyes moved from her mother's face to her daughter's, causing her to feel nauseous. The headache was at its strongest now. "I gotta lay down. Here!" she said while harshly shoving the partially wet spoon at Brooke. "You love her so much; make sure she eats." Storming through the kitchen, she purposely bumped into Ashanti, nearly causing her to fall, before reaching her bedroom and slamming the door behind her. Looking around, she zoned in on the crayon marks on the wall on the room's right side before bringing her attention to the hole that sat on the opposite side. Her bed consisted of only a mattress, a fitted sheet that didn't quite fit, and an old worn-out blanket.

"I hate this place!" She huffed. "I hate my life!" Flopping down on the floor, she leaned her back against the hole in the wall and put her head in her hands as thoughts of Donald crept into her mind. *That bitch better pay me my money. I did what he asked me to do, and he won't pay me.* Turning, she repositioned herself to lay flat on her stomach, using her hands as a pillow, while thoughts continued to take over. Blood emerged, causing her nausea to level out at an even ten. *The kid didn't deserve that. I guess I should've at least called the police and got the kid some help.* Turning her head to the opposite side, her mind began to replay the moments after she shot into the car.

The child sat in the front passenger seat, fiddling with a toy firetruck. She watched as her hands trembled with both excitement and fear as the child was slumped over. He looked as if he'd just fallen asleep rather than being shot, aside from the blood and its splatter. Her eyes danced from the kid to the house and then back at the kid before quickly grabbing one of his hands, the closest that was easiest to reach and placing it around the gun. She shuttered at how small his hands were compared to the gun. The air was crisp, and the rainfall that day was cold, making it difficult to run completely away from the house before people emerged. Dodging behind a withered rose bush that sat in the far left of the yard, she watched her professor sprint to the car first. Followed by a woman, no doubt was the child's mother and her intended target, as she let out a scream that would make the deadliest serial killer drop their head down in shame. Sitting up, she wiped the small tear that had fallen and leaned her head back against the wall.

"Heather?"

Looking over at the door, Heather frowned. *I hate her ass.* "What?!"

"The rice is ready, but there's nothing else in the fridge to cook with it. What were you planning—"

"Nothing! Just rice."

"Huh? What ya mean, *just* rice?"

"I said…" Sighing loudly, Heather rushed to the door and whipped it open. "Rice! That's all she gets tonight." Glaring at Ashanti, she pursed her lips at the tiny freckles that lined her face before moving her eyes to Ashanti's long black curly hair. *Looking just like that whore of a grandmother she has. Only difference is that bitch's hair is blonde, and her eyes are blue. Out of all the people you could've took after, it's your damn grandmother. Maybe if you'd looked more like me and your grandfather, hell, even your wack-ass father, I'd like you more.*

Ashanti looked up at her mother, staring innocently and a bit confused.

"Get out of my face!" Heather yelled.

Startled, Ashanti jumped and moved over towards Brooke.

"You know, Heather, you need to stop treating Ashanti like she's trash. What kind of a mother yells at her daughter that way?"

"What kind of mother walks away from her daughter?"

Brooke slowly nodded her head and grabbed Ashanti's left hand. "I'm not going into this with you again, Heather. You know why I left you with your father because you were sick, and from what I'm seeing here tonight, you still are."

Heather remained quiet as her mother gave her speech.

"I did what I felt was best for you; your father and I felt you should live with him, so that's what we did. You were a child, and that's it. Now, you're more than welcome to spend time with my family and me but don't come over there if you're in one of your moods. I'm taking my granddaughter out of here; you can come and visit, but she will be staying with us."

Heather continued to remain quiet as the feeling of relief gripped her. *Finally getting her ass out of here. Now, maybe I can have a life.*

"Ashanti, go and get your favorite toys and your coat. It's snowing and cold out there."

"Okay!" Ashanti yelped.

Brooke shook her head while she grabbed her purse, retrieved her car keys, and tapped the automatic start button. "You have nothing to say?"

Heather smirked at her mother, "Nope."

"Ha! Go figure. A thank you would be nice."

Heather folded her arms and slanted her head. Brooke sucked her teeth and chuckled. "Okay," she muttered.

"Ashanti? Come on, baby, we got some chili at home and some fresh baked cookies!"

Ashanti reemerged with her jacket and her flip-flops and a jacket that was just as thin as a sheet of notebook paper. "Ready!" She smiled with her arms opened wide, proud that she'd dressed herself.

"Where's your coat, Sweetie? It's cold," Brooke quivered for emphasis.

"Right here," Ashanti laughed.

Brooke looked over at Heather, and Heather shrugged her shoulders.

"Come on, baby, the heat is on in the car. First thing tomorrow, we'll go out and get you a real coat."

Heather casually walked over to the door and opened it, bringing the cold and snow into the house. Brooke picked Ashanti up and quickly walked out of the house. Turning to give Heather one last goodbye, Brooke was met with a viciously slammed door in her and Ashanti's face.

CHAPTER 5

How 'bout some coffee?"

Preston opened his eyes to see Donald standing in front of him, smiling and holding a small green plastic coffee mug with the words *Golden's Joy* plastered on the front.

"Don?"

"Yeah, I figured you haven't had anything to eat or drink since being here, so I thought I'd start you off with some fresh coffee. Got it from the cafeteria down—"

"Where you been?" Instantly annoyed, Preston sat up in his seat.

"I went home to get you some clean clothes, but when I got there, I laid down for a bit only to wake up hours later. I was planning on coming back, but I guess I was overly tired."

Preston stood up. "I don't want no coffee," he said before stomping away from Donald. Looking over at the nurses' station, Preston cleared his throat. He wiped his eyes, working to erase any residuals of his sleep before walking over to the desk. The crew was different than the ones who were there previously.

"Yes, sir, can I help you?"

"Uh, yeah, please. My son... Jordan. How... How is he doing?"

"I'll see if I can get a nurse out here for you." The receptionist said.

"Thanks." Preston nodded.

"Why don't you go home for a while? I'll stay here with—"

"Hell no! You couldn't even stay here with me last night. You think I'm gonna let you sit here with Jordan? Nah, you got me all the way messed up."

"Preston, I—"

"You what, Don? Huh? You left and didn't even let me know you were leaving! You just dipped on me!"

"Yeah, and I—"

Preston slung his right hand up, quieting Donald. "I got it from here. You can go on home, and we can link up later."

Donald sat the coffee cup on the corner of the round desk that sat at the nurses' station. "Alright, I'll see you at home. Kiss Jor—"

Again, Preston lifted his right hand in irritation as he kept his eyes focused on the nurses' station.

"Okay then," Donald responded in a bit of a harsh tone before quickly walking away.

Looking over his shoulder, Preston waved him off, turning all of his attention on the nurse who stood in front of him. "My son," he hoarsely said.

"Yep, follow me. I'll take you back."

"Becca, I'll be right back."

"Come on, Mr. Dixon. It is Mr. Dixon, correct?"

"Yes, ma'am."

The nurse moved quickly over to the enormous electronic door to which Dr. Haven walked in and out as he brought new updates. The door that brought anxiety and fear to Preston each and every time it sounded the click; the signal that someone deemed important was coming out from behind it.

A strong wave of nausea grabbed Preston's stomach, pulling and tugging hard at him. Following behind the nurse, he looked over at the wall on his left and then over to his right. The bright colors that were once there all seemed to blend in together, creating a blurred mess. The sour taste of vomit began to move from the bottom of his stomach and up his esophagus. Coughing, he abruptly stopped and threw both hands up to his mouth. He tilted his head back, hoping to catch the empty stomach contents before he made a foodless mess all over the hospital's floor. A long rectangular door greeted Preston and the nurse. The nurse popped her nametag up from the bottom of her jacket and slung it over the small silver sensor that sat to the left of the rectangular door. The door slowly opened, bringing on a new, forceful wave of nausea. Glancing around, he noticed numbers on each of the doors, all having last names and a letter beside them; he assumed the abbreviation stood for the patient's first name.

"You doing okay?" The nurse glanced back at Preston. "Can I get you something to drink or anything?"

"Nah, I'm okay," he managed to stammer out before taking notice of a tiny being, lying in bed, with a large tube connected to his face and to a massive machine that beeped uncontrollably. *Oh God*, he breathed noiselessly as the nurse continued to walk through the hall, greeting fellow nurses who were in view. Passing by and on to the next rooms that held sick and injured children, the vision of the long white tube burned Preston's thoughts, bringing him to the beginning of what he felt was a meltdown.

"Mr. Dixon?"

"Yeah?" Preston mumbled.

"Are you sure you're okay? Can I get you some water?"

"Um," he began as he leaned all his weight on the wall closest to him.

"Whoa! Hey… Diane, can you grab me a wheelchair, please?"

"Nah… I-I'm good. I just need a few minutes, that's all." Preston placed his left hand on the wall to steady himself while using his right hand to keep anything from falling out of his mouth. The nurse gently rubbed his back while two other nurses stood beside him for extra comfort and precaution.

"Maybe we can go back and try again later."

Preston stood up taller, gathering himself the best he could before slowly locking eyes with the nurse. "No, I'm alright. My son needs me."

The nurse remained quiet as Preston continued to gather himself. Standing completely, he mustered a smile and nodded at each of the staff before turning to his guide. "I'm ready," he said in a voice full of forced and rushed confidence.

"Alright, he's right over here." The nurse moved to the room just a few feet away from where they were standing. Taking in a long deep breath, Preston joined her and slowly peeped in. His eyes fell on the thick white bandage that laced the top of the child's head. Gasping, he turned away from the child, his child that no longer looked like he was supposed to. The cute, small round face that resembled Stephanie's and a touch of his was no more. Instead, Preston saw a fuller, chubbier, swollen face. Both big and small, tubes and machines, were close to his bed. Soft, joyful music serenaded the room from the medium-sized cartoon character-designed TV that sat in the room's upper right corner. To Preston's sanity, the machines were quiet, keeping him at a superficial sense of peace.

"Mr. Dixon?"

"Hmmm?" Preston jolted at the sound of the nurse's voice. For some reason, her words were muffled, but he responded to her anyway. "Yes?" Thankful for the interruption, he turned away from Jordan and gave his full attention to the nurse.

"Can I get you something? We have bottled water in the fridge. Or maybe some coffee?"

His nose began to fill, and his eyes felt misty. "Uh…" His mind overpowered his body, bringing forward a robust urge to turn back towards his bruised and bandaged child. Wiping his nose with the back of his hand, he cautiously walked over to Jordan. The monitor above the bed chirped, temporarily stopping Preston's breath. Holding his breath tight, he began to feel faint, and his feet began to feel light.

"Mr. Dixon, why don't you sit next to him." Pulling the recliner that sat in the far right of the room, near the window, closer to Preston, the nurse grabbed two pillows from the closet and tucked them firmly onto it. "Here you go," she gently said as she patted the seat. "Talk to him. Let him know you are here."

Preston looked away from Jordan, then to the nurse before fixing his eyes to land on Jordan again. Keeping them there, he slowly sat down in the chair. His small body was

57

plumper than he was used to seeing him, and his eyes were shut tight with a sappy-looking substance in the corner of each of them.

"Don't cry, Jordan."

"Huh?" The nurse was puzzled at Preston's first words to his son.

Preston quickly turned to the nurse and pointed at Jordan. "He has tears in his eyes," he whispered.

Walking over to Preston, she gently patted him on the shoulder before grabbing a small blue and white tube with a silver cap from off the counter. Looking up at the small whiteboard that sat above the counter, she tilted her head towards the door. *Tabitha*, she mumbled as she unscrewed the cap off the tube.

"Hey, is Tabitha out there?" Moving closer to the door, she leaned against it. "Mary?"

"Yeah?"

"Is Tabitha out there?"

"No, she walked a patient to CT."

"Oh, okay."

Walking back over to the counter, she placed the tube back in its space before swiftly pulling the bottom portion of the counter outwards. *Let me see…*

Preston glanced behind his shoulder before refocusing his eyes on Jordan. *His face is so swollen.* Images of Stephanie emerged in his mind, replacing his sadness with anger. The nurse's quick tapping soothed his anger a bit. Knowing that someone besides him cared enough for Jordan to help him brought comfort. In his mind, the nurse's typing was her effort to find more information on Jordan.

"Okay, so he gets the ointment on his eyes every two hours. Tabitha just put some on his eyes, so that's what we see, not tears. An ointment to keep his eyes moistened and healthy.

Preston nodded his head. "Thank you."

"You're very welcome. I like to explain things to our families. This stuff can seem so foreign when you're not used to seeing it."

Preston nodded and watched as the nurse closed the computer, slid it back in its space, and moved throughout the room, placing objects and materials in neater positions. *Jaime*, he read the name next to the picture on her badge that fell loosely from a small round pin attached to her jacket. *I'll send her a gift or something once Jordan is out of here.*

"I'll leave you two alone for a wh—"

"No… please stay. I-I'm not used to seeing my son…."

"Yes, I understand."

Words were jumbled and crammed into Preston's mind, like a pretzel freshly wrapped at a county fair. He struggled to form them well enough to bring a coherent word, let alone a full sentence. "I just—"

"It's okay, no explanation needed," Jaime said as she pulled the other chair from across the room and sat down next to Preston. "Cute lil fella."

Preston smiled, "Thank you." Reaching over, he slowly placed his left hand on the bed, careful not to actually touch any part of Jordan's body.

"It's alright. Go ahead, hold his hand."

Glancing at Jaime, Preston reluctantly followed the nurse's orders and moved his hand closer.

"Go on," she soothed.

Preston inhaled before exhaling and then placed his hand on top of Jordan's. It was cold and clammy, causing him to slightly jump back. "Um, maybe we should get him a blanket," he mumbled.

"Yep, let's grab a nice warm blanket. Fresh out of the warmer." Jaime hopped up from the chair. "A nice warm blanket. Would you like one too? It is a little chilly in here. Most of the rooms are."

"No, thank you," he replied as he kept his eyes on Jordan's hands. "His hands…" The beginning folds of his cry were at bay, bringing him to complete silence. The first tear fell right before the doctor walked in.

"Mr. Dixon, hi there."

Preston nodded while Jaime retrieved a packet of tissues from her pocket. "I'll be right back with that blanket," she said before smacking the sanitizer nozzle and exiting the room.

"Hi," Preston said through a moderate sniffle. He lifted his head enough to see a team of people, all standing behind Dr. Haven. Putting his head back down, he listened as the doctor ruffled through some papers.

"We're gonna take a quick look."

Preston remained quiet as the people surrounded the bed. Standing, he moved over towards the door and turned away.

"Jordan, hey bud. It's Dr. Haven. I'm just gonna take a quick listen to ya."

Wait, he can hear? Preston's mind was now at a full-blown ten.

"Jordan, can you wiggle your—?"

"He can hear?"

All eyes were now on Preston, bringing him to a deep, uncomfortable state.

Dr. Haven smiled. "We like to believe he can. We turned his sedation down a bit earlier this morning, so we are hoping that his body tolerates it and he's able to interact with us a little more. We are..."

The tears were fully falling now as the doctor spoke. No longer able to hear words himself, he leaned against the wall and allowed his body to react. Panic attacks, as his temporary therapist called them when his father died, causing him to go into total adjustment disorder with depression mixed with anxiety.

"Maybe we can…."

Preston inhaled a big breath of air before letting it out slowly, just as he'd learned in therapy. The doctor's words faded in and out, making it impossible to understand.

"Mr. Dixon?"

"Yeah?"

"Maybe you should sit down."

Preston shook his head. "No…"

"Whoa!" One of the women in the bunch called out. Another rushed the chair that Jamie had previously occupied over to Preston and guided him to the seat.

"Why y'all didn't call me?!"

Preston immediately stood up at the sound of the loud and overbearing tone. A tone he recognized more than he wished he did. Stephanie rushed into the room, being sure to roll her eyes at her ex.

"I should've been in here first!"

Dr. Haven folded his arms while the others nonchalantly gazed. "Well…" he started.

"I don't want nobody in here when y'all are talking 'bout my child! Got it?!"

Preston kept his mouth shut as he continued to work on his breathing techniques. Walking in quickly, a woman, unfamiliar to Preston, stood next to him and patted him on the back.

"Ma'am, if you don't calm down, we're going to call security."

"And who the hell are you?"

The woman shook her head. "I'm *his* nurse, and he doesn't need all the—"

"I'll tell you what *my* child needs."

The team continued to keep their eyes on Stephanie, neither of them saying a word.

"My son, my rules!" she gawked while twisting her upper body around as if she were possessed by some other being.

A slight knock on the door called the crowd's attention, immediately bringing Stephanie's demeanor to a calmer, pleasant one. The tall, muscular policeman walked in and nodded at everyone before turning all his attention on Stephanie.

"Ma'am, come with me, please."

"Huh? For what?!"

"For disturbing the peace!" Preston yelled. His senses were back full force with a fresh serving of rage. "Why you even here?!"

"Sir, I can take it—"

"Nah! I'm sick of her mess!" Preston snarled.

"Sir?"

"I'm gonna have to ask everyone to leave!" Jordan's nurse said sternly.

Preston glanced at his son before his eyes landed on Dr. Haven. He began to feel ashamed, not only of himself but of Stephanie as well. Sighing, he slowly dropped his head. "I'm sorry. We shouldn't be in here acting this way."

Lifting his head, he saw sympathy, which to him was unexpected but greatly appreciated.

"Why don't we schedule a meeting? Let's talk in the conference room. Say... uh... today at around twelve-thirty or—"

"Nope! We can talk right here!"

Preston moved his eyes on Stephanie, opened his mouth, but swiftly changed his mind. *No need.*

"Ma'am, if you don't come with me right now, I'll have to forcefully remove you, and none of us want that."

Preston peeped over at his son again before placing his eyes on Stephanie and the police officer, instantly becoming a spectator, just as the others. Stephanie lifted her hands and stormed out of the room; the security guard nodded at the crew before following her.

"Um…" Preston began. I want to—"

"It's alright, Mr. Dixon."

Preston nodded, "Thanks, Doc."

Preston watched as Dr. Haven fiddled with the machines. Simultaneously, one of the other people in his camp manipulated the medicines hanging on the long silver pole before scribbling something on a notepad.

"Let's move it to twenty," she quietly said to everyone. The team clicked their pens and began writing. Dr. Haven pushed one of the buttons on the machine before turning to Preston.

"Looks like's he's doing alright today. We are going to decrease his sedation, but we are restricting visitors to one at a time. You understand that we—"

"Yes, I understand, Doctor, thank you."

Dr. Haven nodded before walking around a few people, shaking Preston's hand, and walking out the door. The team followed close behind him, leaving him alone with Jordan. *A damn shame*, he mumbled before looking out at the crowd gathered around the nurse, who was rapidly typing. Looking over at Jordan, Preston forced all thoughts of Stephanie out of his mind before he began to pray.

CHAPTER 6

What up, Ma?!"

"Chadbert! Do you have to slam the door every time you come over?"

"What up, Pops?" Chad chuckled. "My bad."

"Yeah, it's your bad."

Chad laughed aloud as he walked into the den, turned she-cave to greet his mother. "What up, ma," he said before kissing her on the cheek.

"Hey, baby. How you doing? How's Ms. Annie?"

"I'm good. Ms. Annie's good. I think she's going to be going home today."

"Oh good, thank heavens! I'm so glad she's doing better. Yeah. So... what you cook?"

"Ha, nothing. You know I don't cook all the time now. Not since you moved out."

"What? Ah, come on Ma; you still got Pops and AJ to—"

"Nope, your daddy got his leftovers, and I keep the freezer full for AJ. The only one who just had to have a hot home-cooked meal was you!"

Chad flopped down on his mother's massage chair and flipped the power button on. He glanced at his mother in hopes she had her *"Get out of my chair"* annoyed look on her face just so he could get his laugh on. To his surprise, she flipped her chair to recliner mode, not bothering to argue a word.

Grabbing the extra remote, Chad pressed buttons on it until he reached The Zone, a station that aired nothing but sports. An old football game replaced his mother's favorite talk show, a show she made sure to watch each and every day.

"Hey!"

"Yeah, I knew that would get you going." Laughing, he adjusted the speed to moderate on the chair. Immediately, the mechanical balls rotated faster, simultaneously hitting all of his tension areas. "Man, this thing do work."

He chuckled as his mother pushed her feet down to move the bottom of her chair in its rightful position, stood up, and stretched. "You know better than to turn my show."

Popping Chad on the hand, she snatched the remote from him and tapped the previous channel button…

Right! We have to learn and know that it's our responsibility to look out for our own feelings and thoughts. The audience rang out in applause before another one of the hosts jumped in to speak.

"You and your talk shows."

"Yep, you know I love me some ChiChat. Those girls be dropping some gems."

"Yeah, we know Ma," Chad shook his head and closed his eyes. He allowed the mechanical fingers to relax him while trying his hardest to block out the women talking on the TV.

You gotta let kids live their own lives. We all had our time, so now, we gotta let our children go, no matter how hard it is. Another round of applause erupted.

"That's right! Hmph! Got to let them go, no matter how ha—"

"Ma, she just said that."

"So, I can… Why are you still here? Speaking of letting kids go, I'm starting with you! Well, your sister was first, and now you!"

A small cry from the living room snatched Chad's attention.

"She finally woke up."

"The baby here?"

"Yeah, I went and got her last night. I think she caught a cold from being out there in the snow and that cold air without a coat."

"Why she ain't have a—"

"Her mama and her mess. You know all she had was a jacket? As cold as it is outside."

Chad shook his head before sitting up in the chair and clicking the power button off. He watched as his mother slid her feet in her slippers. "Ma… Stop."

"What?"

"ChiChat slippers?"

"Yeah… and…?"

Chad hopped out of the chair and waited for his mother to exit first before following her.

"Come on, baby. Let Grandma clean that nose off."

"Hey ma-ma," Chad said softly. "Come here." Picking his niece up, he kissed her on the cheek before sitting down on the couch and placing her in his lap.

"My head houts."

"Your head?"

"Yeah, my head houts."

"Tell Grandma where it hurts, Ashanti."

"Right heah." Ashanti responded as she pointed to the back of her head before laying it down on Chad's chest.

"Might be all those bows and mess on her head. Take some of them thangs out my baby head, Brooke."

Brooke sat down next to Chad and Ashanti. "Yeah, Alvin, you might be right."

"I don't know why that girl put all dem bows on that baby head."

"Uh-huh, 'cause they pretty," Brooke said while she unloosened the orange balls and unwrapped the braid, freeing Ashanti's hair.

Chad looked down at Ashanti and smiled. "Feel better?"

"No," Ashanti answered before coughing a chest-rattling cough.

"Uh oh, it might be more than just bows, Pop."

"Yeah, with that mama she got, it could be anything."

Brooke lightly chuckled as she continued to remove the marble-shaped blue and white bows and barrettes off Ashanti's hair.

"What was she doing out in the cold without a coat anyway?"

"Uh, you know how Heather can be. Just as mean as a rattlesnake. Especially towards this baby. Let me go out and get her something for her runny nose and nasty cough."

"Nah, Ma, I got it. I got to get ready to go over to Madisyn's house. I can stop at the store real quick before I go. Looks like it's getting ready to snow again."

"Look at you. Being all re-spon-sible."

Chuckling, Chad handed Ashanti off to Brooke before grabbing his coat and throwing it on. "I'll be right back. Aye, AJ!' He hollered upstairs to his brother.

"You know he up there playing that game."

"Or either on the phone. Got 'em a little girlfriend now."

"Oh, word?" Chad giggled. "My lil bro."

Brooke nodded her head slowly as Alvin proudly slid out a sly grin.

"Looks like I need to chill wit' him. See was sup wit' him."

Alvin blindly flipped through the channels while Brooke rubbed her hands through Ashanti's hair.

"AJ!" Chad walked closer to the stairs. "AAAAA-J!"

"Huh?! What?!" AJ yelled from his bedroom through the closed door.

Chad laughed, making sure to laugh loudly as he heard AJ's room door open forcefully, purposefully casting annoyance.

"Huh?"

"You wanna go to the store wit' me?"

"Nah, I'm good."

Nodding his head, Chad zipped his coat and opened the front door. "Damn...that damn snow again... Um... dang..." Looking over at his mother, he smiled. Sorry, ma."

"Uh-huh, you know better than to use that language while you're in front of me."

"Yes, ma'am," he laughed. "It's snowing again."

"They said it's supposed to snow all week," Alvin said while continuing to turn to each station accessible to him. "Ya'll act like this ain't what it do round here. We always get snow."

"Yeah, but not this much, this early," Brooke added before sitting back further on the couch.

"As far as I can remember," Alvin said as he continued to fumble with the TV stations.

"I'll be…" squinting, Chad opened the storm door and focused his eyes on the figure that stood in the yard. The sky was dark, causing him to have to strain his eyes to see. Moving back into the house, he smacked the button to his right, shining a bright light throughout the entire yard. Snow began to fall harder, and the figure continued to hold its place.

"What's the matter?"

"Somebody standing…" Walking onto the porch, he allowed the storm door to slam shut. "Who dat?!" The figure moved a tad off to the right while maintaining its stance.

"Where's my daughter?!" The voice growled.

"Chad, what is it?!"

"Aw… shit… that damn Heather." Chad hissed under his breath. "Ma, it's Heather! Standing out here in the snow, looking STUPID!"

"I got yo' stupid!"

"Oh hell, that girl better get her ass out my yard before I do some poppin' off up in here!"

"Alvin… no!" Brooke said as she stood up, sat Ashanti down in the chair, and rushed off to the door. She looked back at Ashanti before opening the storm door and stepping her right foot onto the cold porch. *Shoot*, she mumbled as partially melted snow softened the bottom of her slipper, bringing unwanted moisture to her foot. Sliding back into the house, she kicked off her slippers and slid on the shoes closest to her, her husband's walking sneakers. She reopened the storm door, glanced back into the house at Ashanti, and joined an annoyed and angry Chad.

"Somebody need to beat her ass!"

"Chadbert, I asked you not to—"

"Sorry, ma, but she make me sick. Always startin'…
sh…stuff."

"What is it, Heather? Do you want to come in and
talk like adults?"

"Ma!"

Brooke held up her right hand before folding her
arms in an attempt to shield herself from the cold breeze and
drops of snow that were both attacking her.

"Come on up here. We can—"

"Where is my child?!"

Chad shook his head. "You know what… Let me go.
Ma, I'll be right back with the medicine. And you!" Chad
trotted down the steps, pointing at the unwelcomed visitor.
"Shit. Damn ice!" Grabbing the rail, he stomped his left foot
on the last step to remove the blob of snow he'd stepped on
before stepping down onto the walkway. "You need to get
yo' ass away from here! Go back to the shack you call a
house and—"

"Fuck you, Chad!"

"Nah, you do too much of that already. That's why
you—"

"Chad! Go on to the store!"

"I'll tell you what," Alvin muted the TV, stood up, and walked over to the door. "She better get her ass away from this here house!"

"Alvin…" Brooke held her hand up towards her husband while keeping her eyes on Chad. "Alvin, go back and sit down. I got this. Chad, go on to the store and get the baby's medicine."

Chad walked quickly yet carefully to his car without another word, unlocked the driver's side door, and hopped in. "Why she even over here?" Turning the engine, he lifted himself, pulled his phone out of his pocket, and opened it. A picture of Madisyn popped on the screen, bringing him to a split second of peace before his mind reminded him of the mess that was right outside his window. He clicked the heater button and flipped the windshield wipers on low. Tiny, partially melted snowflakes fell off the windshield and off to the side.

"I'm telling you, lil girl, to get off my property!"

Damn. Chad rolled down his window. "Go back in the house, Pop. Let her ass stay—"

"Chadbert! Go!"

Chad put his foot on the break and moved the gear in reverse. The engine jumped, giving him permission to move the car out of his parents' driveway, away from the drama that was sure to unfold at any given minute. Thinking of Ashanti and her headache, he slowly eased his foot slightly off the brake, allowing the car to remove him and handle Ashanti's medicine business. Glancing at his mother, he frowned at the bewildered look that gripped her face and shook his head at the anger that was all over his father's. Changing focus, he looked through his rearview mirror at the small bands of snow falling lightly that rested on the top of his trunk. His peripheral sight caught a glimpse of his sister, standing with her hands on her hips. *That's one stupid ass girl.* Taking his foot off a little more, the car moved faster. *Thud…*

"Chad!" He heard his mother yell. Slamming down on the break, he peered through the rearview mirror. *What the hell?* Heather was in clear focus now, holding her left leg.

"You hit me!"

What the… Quickly opening his door, Chad sighed loudly. "What the hell?!"

"Why you hit meeeee?!" Heather screamed. Barking from a distance echoed through the air.

Oh, God!" Brooke yelled. "Chaaad!"

"Ma, this bitch jumped in front—"

"I got yo' bitch! I done told you before to stop calling me that!" Heather pounced on Chad, catching him completely off guard. She scratched and clawed at him like a cat that just had water thrown on it.

"Heeeeeeeeeather!" Brooke hollered.

Chad remained still, remembering that his father's number one rule was to never put hands on a woman in anger. No matter the circumstance.

Brooke ran off the porch and screamed, "Stop it!" Sliding on a patch of snow, she kept going through the yard until she reached Heather and pulled her as hard as she could. Both Heather and Brooke fell into the grass. Adrenaline reared heavily through Brooke's body, allowing her to freely slither on the cold, wet ground. "Stop it, Heather!"

Heather pulled Brooke's hair, causing her to yelp out in pain and surprise. Reacting, Brooke slapped Heather hard on the face.

"Yo!" Chad roared. Running towards the fight, he reached to grab his mother off of Heather when a gunshot stopped him in his tracks. Ducking down, he looked towards the porch to see his father standing there, aiming his shotgun in the air.

"Now I told you to get yo' ass out my yard! This is my house, and you will not bring yo' ass here and disrespect it!"

All eyes were on Alvin as he shot another shot in the air. More barks from the neighbors' dogs rang out, piercing the night's sky. Heather pushed Brooke off her while Chad pulled.

"Come on, Ma, she ain't worth it."

Brooke allowed Chad to guide her up. An enraged Heather sprang to her feet and ran off into the darkness of the night. Both Chad and Brooke watched until Heather was out of close view.

"I don't know why you keep dealing with her."

"She's my daughter, Chadbert. I gotta—"

"No, Ma, that don't matter. If she's going to be disrespectful, then you don't need her around."

Chad held his mother's hand as they both walked towards the porch. Alvin opened the door and walked into the house, holding the door open for his family to join him. Suddenly, the light snow falling changed to a thick, heavier shower, swiftly covering the yard and the first two steps. *Don't make no sense*, Chad mumbled as he stopped to allow his mother to walk in first before he followed.

CHAPTER 7

Throwing his hat on the couch, Preston deeply inhaled and slowly exhaled as the sweet aroma of pine and apples engulfed his home, giving his nose a much-needed break from the smell of alcohol and disinfectant. *So good to be home.* He looked back at Madisyn as she sat in her car, on the phone, giddy about the hottest tea Chad was spilling about his estranged sister. Closing the door, he instinctively clicked the lock upwards, locking himself in and Madisyn out. Looking over at the coffee table, a picture of Jordan smiled a gap-filled smile back at him. *Huh, when he lost his two front teeth.* Taking off his sweater, he threw it next to his hat, placed his keys on the rack next to the door, and headed to the kitchen. *Damn, Maddy still out there.* Turning back towards the living room, he glanced at Jordan's picture and quickly rushed to the door to unlock it. Opening the storm door, the chill of winter brushed over his body, bringing him to a shudder. Closing it back, he shook his head and reopened it, deciding to leave it ajar. Walking out of the living room and into the kitchen, he pulled his phone out of his pocket before pulling a stool from underneath the island. *Jordan.*

Opening his contacts, he clicked the nurses' station number and listened as the recorded greeting kindly greeted him. Allowing the woman's voice to soothe him, as he was looking for anything to use that would relieve at least an inch of stress, he used his free hand to massage his neck. Moving his hand up and down on the tightest areas, he waited for someone to answer his call. Removing his hand from his neck, he slid his hand across the phone's speak button and placed the phone on the table before putting both hands around his neck as he massaged deeper. *I know they all got to be—*

"Nurses' Station B! Angela speaking. How may I help you?"

"Uh… Hi… this is Preston. Preston Dixon and I'm calling to check on my son…."

"Damn, it's cold in here! You need to turn on—"

Preston quickly lifted his left hand towards his sister.

"My son, Jordan… Jordan Dixon."

"Hold, please."

Preston turned to his sister. "Checking on Jordan…"

Madisyn nodded before pulling a chair out at the table and sat down. Preston kept his eyes on Madisyn as she strolled through her phone. *Her and social media*, he mumbled. Madisyn chuckled but kept her eyes fixed on the screen.

Moving his hands off his neck again, he picked up his phone and tapped the speaker button again, turning it off. "Uh-huh, I'm here. Yeah, Jordan Dix… Okay… Thanks." Clicking off the phone, Preston slung it on the counter and dropped his head in his hands.

"What?"

"Still the same. On that damn machine. They can't wake him up."

Madisyn put her phone down on the table. "Well, he shot himself in the stomach. And then he's only a child. We should thank God he's…."

Preston swiftly lifted his head and gave Madisyn a death grip of a stare, being sure to keep his eyes locked directly onto hers.

"Sorry… I was just—"

"Got it! Thanks!"

The room grew silent, Preston from anger and Madisyn from embarrassment. Feeling bad at the apparent look of hurt on his sister's face, Preston cleared his throat and stood up. Walking over to the thermostat, he pushed the heater button until it reached seventy-six degrees.

"How's Mama doing?" He asked, hoping a chat about their mother would be the conversation that lightened the heavy cloud that lingered.

Madisyn looked up while twiddling her thumbs. "She good, waiting for you to come over."

"Yeah," Preston said as he walked over to the coffee maker and opened the coffee bean dispenser. "I'll stop by after I take a shower; before I go back to the hospital."

"Yep, she's home, resting. Trying her hardest to get in the kitchen and cook something."

Preston snickered while grabbing a coffee filter and pouring fresh-ground coffee into it.

"Why do you still use that old thing? You need to get with the rest of us and use what we use. You ain't even gotta do all that; just pop a flavor in, some water and—"

"Right," Preston mumbled as he slid the coffee holder in its rightful position and flipped on the cold water. "Got it!" he turned and smiled at his sister before completing the last step to making his coffee. Leaning against the counter, he focused his attention on Madisyn. *She looks so much older now.*

"What?"

"Nothing, just looking. What? I can't look at my lil sister?"

"Not if you 'bout to go into some sort of lecture. I am not one of your English students at Townsend Pines University." Madisyn playfully rolled her eyes.

"TPU is fine. Why you gotta be all formal? Or, in your case, sarcastic," Preston laughed.

Both Preston and Madisyn busied themselves in their own personal affairs, amplifying the kitchen clock's tick. Gurgling from the coffee maker soon joined the clock's hum and filled the house's silence. Preston stood up and stretched. *Donald*, he accidentally muttered, hoping that Madisyn didn't catch what he'd said.

"Yeah, where is he? I haven't seen him since Thanksgiving."

Damn, of course, she did. The problem is, I don't know where his ass is either. "Uh... working."

Madisyn flipped her brother the side-eye and picked up her phone. "Right."

"What's that supposed to mean?"

"Nothing, nothing at all. I was just agreeing. What's wrong with you? You seem jumpy... jumpy at everything somebody says to you."

"Jumpy? Nah, just a lot on my mind. You know, with Jordan being in the hospital and Mama—"

"And *Donald.*"

"No, Donald is way on the last of my list of concerns."

"Mm-hmm."

Preston turned from Madisyn, grabbed a small coffee mug from the cup rack, and poured his coffee into it. The steam of the coffee smacked his nose, bringing a satisfied smirk to his face. "Now, this is coffee. That mess they have at the hospital ain't nothing compared to this."

Madisyn nodded and stood up. "Well, I gotta go. Chad's on his way to the house. His mother baked a pie for Mama so—"

"Oh, that's nice."

"Yeah, she's pretty nice."

Preston nodded his head before taking a sip of his coffee.

"Ugh! You ain't going to put nothing in that?"

"Nope, black is the best," he replied as he put the cup to his lips. "This is how to do it."

"Hmmm," Madisyn frowned. "What time you coming by the house?"

"I'm going to go and take my shower now and then head over right after. I want to get back over to the hospital before it gets too late."

"Oh yeah, what time is visiting hours?"

"I don't have visiting hours. They let me come and go as many times as I want."

"Oh, okay, that's good. And Stephanie? I know you ain't trying to be around her."

Preston swallowed a longer sip of his drink and nodded his head. "Wack bitch ain't allowed in there without security after she had her little *tantrum*."

"Humph, why am I not surprised?"

Preston shook his head and placed his mug on the counter. "I'll be over there shortly. Let me get my ass in the shower."

"Yeah, yo' stankin' ass."

"I'mma let that slide... 'cause you right. Only 'cause you are right."

Madisyn chuckled and walked out of the kitchen and into the living room. "I'll let Mama know you coming over. See you later."

"K!" Preston called out. Waiting to hear the door slam, he went into his bedroom and flopped down on the bed. Sighing, he glanced over at Donald's side of the bed and rolled his eye. *Maybe we've run our course.* Laying back, he closed his eyes. Donald's lips entered his mind first, followed by his perfect, straight white teeth and then his complete smile. Preston kept his eyes closed as the picture of Donald before all the trouble and negativity froze itself in his brain. Then, the sight of the arguments, jealous rants, and all his disappearances, when his presence mattered most, gripped his mind. Quickly, the blood popped in, right before a limp Jordan harshly threw itself in the mix. Preston swiftly opened his eyes and sat up. *Damn. Ah, damn it, man.* The sound of the door opening removed all other thoughts from his mind. Standing, he walked out of his bedroom to see Donald walking through the living room.

"Well, look who it is! You finally—"

"Not now, Preston."

Preston stood still as Donald rushed past him and went straight to the bathroom. The bathroom door slammed shut, and the shower was immediately started. Leaving Preston both confused and angry.

CHAPTER 8

U
gh!" Stephanie screamed loudly while throwing the last of the pictures on the floor. A mess of shattered glass rested at her feet while rage clutched her heart. Slowing her breathing, her eyes caught glimpses of Preston's mangled face through the broken pieces of the frames. *I hate him, but I love him too. How is that even possible?* She allowed her body to slide from the arm of the couch and onto the floor as tears fell. *I don't get it! Damn, I just don't—*

"Get up off that floor! Whatchu doing down there?"

Stephanie rolled her eyes and quickly hopped up on her bare feet, careful not to step in the glass. "I was just—"

"Just nothing! You sitting in here while your child is lying in the hospital with a bullet in his belly, and your man is still parading around with his *boyfriend*! You don't have the luxury of just sitting here... having tantrums!" Janet shook her head in disgust at the pile of glass on the floor. "Clean this mess up!"

Without hesitation, Stephanie grabbed the broom and dustpan. *This my house. How she gonna come up in here and tell me what to do?* She began sweeping the mess. Picking up the picture, she smiled as she and Preston stared back at her. *The happy times.* Placing it on the table, she readied the broom again and began sweeping.

"Uh-uh! Rip that picture up and throw it in the pile!"

"What?" Stephanie looked over at her mother, confused about her demand.

"You heard me! If you can't be woman enough to keep your man, then you don't need pictures of him around the house. How can you be so unfulfilling that you allow a *man* to steal your man away?"

Stephanie maneuvered her lips to speak, but no words were formed as usual when it came to her mother. She remained quiet and did as she was told. Slicing the 5 x 7 picture into two, she looked over at her mother. *Satisfied, bitch?*

"More! Into shreds!" Janet yelled while dropping down on the couch. "No telling when you'll have a weak moment and tape the thing up. You need to make sure it's ripped up good so you can't mend it! Not until you mend the actual relationship."

Anger formed in the pit of Stephanie's stomach as she ripped the picture into tiny pieces, throwing them onto the floor and into the pile with the glass.

"Yeah, that's better."

"Mama, you…" She stopped herself and held all her anger inside as she tightly gripped the broom and began sweeping the pile into the dustpan.

Flipping over on his left side, Donald slowly opened his eyes to see Preston's side of the bed empty, a sight he's been used to seeing over the past few days. He raised his arms into a long stretch before sitting up in bed.

"Preston?!" Waiting for a reply, he slid his body completely out from underneath the covers and rubbed his feet on the carpeted floor.

"Preston?!" He called out louder. Again, he was met with silence. *I guess he's already gone to the hos…* **BOOM… BOOM… BOOM…**

Jumping up, he rushed to the open bedroom door and peered out. *Who the hell is that knocking like they the police?*

BOOM... BAM... BAM... BAM...

Angry, he threw on his robe, stormed out of his bedroom, and over to the living room door. "Who the hell is it?!" Deciding not to wait for a response, he forcefully unlocked the door and pulled it open. A disheveled Heather angrily greeted him.

"Are you crazy?! Have you completely lost your mind?"

"Yep, but you know that already! I want my money now!"

Donald wrapped his robe tightly around his body to shield himself from not only the frigid temperature of the early morning cold but from Heather's icy stare as well. "I told you to never come over to my house. Why are you—"

"Because I want my money now! Give me my money, or I'll go in that cozy lil house of yours and blow up the entire—"

Donald used his elbow and his hip as a stand to keep the door slightly open, a barrier to keep Heather out of his house. "Well, lucky for me, nobody's here, so...."

Heather placed her hands on her hips and groaned loudly.

"Now I told you before that I'm not paying you for a job that you didn't do. I'm just not gonna do—"

"UGH! Somebody help me! This man is attacking me! Help, I—"

"Shut up!" Donald howled in a tone a tad above a whisper.

Heather smirked as she glanced at the surrounding houses. They were as empty, appearing as they've been when she first walked up to Donald's door. Unsatisfied, she sucked in a gulp of air and prepared to scream, much louder than before.

"Alright!" Donald hissed as he reached out to grab Heather, but she quickly stepped back and threw her hands up, readying herself for a fight.

"Put your damn hands down. Ain't nobody gonna p—"

"You better not put your hands on me!"

Donald eyed his neighborhood as he let go of the door and joined Heather on the porch. "I'll send you some money soon. Just go."

"How soon?"

"Today! Now go!" He begged through gritted teeth. Donald watched anxiously as Heather hopped down the steps and made her way out into the yard. He waited until she was on her way out of the yard and halfway down the street before he went back into the house. Closing his eyes, he nodded his head and leaned against the wall. Opening his eyes slowly, he blankly surveyed the living room. In pure disbelief that Heather was willing to go to such lengths as yelling out lies that she was in danger. That she would really cry wolf, in his neighborhood, around the people who've called him neighbor and friend for years. Thoughts of Chris moved around in his head, along with the thought of being blackmailed by Chris' daughter. *All that I've done for that girl, and she treats me like this.* Shutting his eyes again, he sighed heavily while rubbing both temples. *I took care of her when her mother left and abandoned her. This is the thanks I...*

"Hey."

Popping his eyes open, he turned quickly to see Preston standing in the doorway. "Preston!"

"Yeah?"

Oh, shoot, how much did he hear? I thought he was gone. "I-I… I thought you were gone to the hospital. I didn't know—"

"Oh, nah. I was out back."

Donald watched in fear and nervousness as Preston sat down on the couch and laid his head against the middle cushion.

Donald stood still, waiting on the questions to begin. *I guess I'll just tell him that she's my niece. Nah… not niece… maybe…*

Preston looked up. "What? Trying to figure out what I'm thinking?"

Shit! He does know! Although his robe was wrapped comfortably, he pulled the tightening strings a bit more as the warmth of the robe calmed the shiver that was taking place within his body. He watched intently as Preston's face changed from irritation to anger. A look that he'd recognized from his teenage days. The menacing and intimidating look

101

that his greatest opponents had before they lifted their fist to sucker punch him.

"Don?"

"Uh… I was just—"

"I hope you were just going to tell me—"

"Just a family friend," Donald blurted out.

"What?" Preston frowned.

"Huh?" Donald quipped.

"Yo, what is the matter with you? Family friend? Whatchu talkin' bout?"

"Oh," Donald let out an anxious chuckle. "Nothing. I was thinking about something and… well… nevamind." He kept his eyes on Preston, hoping to see a genuine truce and not a look of confusion to which he'd later have to go into more detail about the family friend conversation. Thinking fast, he forced his brain to come up with something to chat about that would help push Preston's look of confusion to a more satisfied, calming one. "Um, how's Jordan?" Moving closer to Preston, he placed his hand on the wall while throwing a look of concern on his face.

"Jordan," Preston said slowly. "Jordan's still laying there. That's just about all I can say about him right now."

Donald nodded his head, not sure what to say to comfort his man. All he could think about was that he knew how Jordan was shot and, most importantly, who actually delivered the shot. Moving off the wall, he reluctantly scooted his feet a few more inches closer to Preston, nervous about touching him as they hadn't touched each other in weeks. *Um*, he mumbled.

"What?" Preston said in a voice filled with irritation.

Donald stopped and gaped his mouth open a bit before he replied. "Nothing, I was just... well... wanted to touch you," he said quickly before dropping his head.

"Really?"

Lifting his head, Donald's emotions transformed from nervousness to a fit of tepid anger at the look of frustration and annoyance on Preston's face. The fury that burned within Preston's eyes gave him a chill causing him to back up.

"I'm sitting here, worried about my son, and you have sex on your mind?"

"What...? Sex? No... I-I was just—"

"Save it, Don. I know when you tryin' to get some, and now is not the time." Preston stood up and folded his arms across his chest. "You know, my son's been in the hospital, fighting for his life, and you have yet to go and see him. But then you call yourself my *man*."

Donald remained quiet as Preston walked slowly out of the room and into the bedroom, slamming the door hard behind him.

CHAPTER 9

S taring at the computer screen, Donald shook his head in hopes of ending the twists and turns of the numbers and letters that sat in a patient's chart on the computer. He took his eyes off the screen and looked towards the window at the end of the hall. Another round of snow fell lightly from the sky, keeping Baltimore as white as a Christmas snow globe. A small group of one of his patients' family members gathered around the window.

"Looks like we'll have to bump up Ten's oxygen. You wanna... Donald? What's wrong?"

"Huh? Oh... nothing," Donald glanced at his friend and fellow physician assistant, Ronnie. "Did you say we need to—"

"Uh-uh, you ain't getting' off that easy. Wassup? Trouble in paradise?"

Donald closed the patient's file and grabbed his laptop off the desk. "No... well..."

"Well?"

"It's nothing. What's the level in Room Ten?"

"Chelsea?"

"Yeah?"

"Come here a minute, please."

Donald placed his left hand under the sanitizer station and waited for the goo to drop. He waved his hand, but nothing came out. *They really need to do better at changing these things*, he murmured.

"Yeah?"

"Hey, Donald."

"Hi. Listen, ya'll need to—"

"Yep, I already sent Michelle to get another bag to refill it."

Donald held his hand up to his forehead. He gave Chelsea a quick salute before walking over to the adjacent nurses' station and placing his laptop down on the desk.

"Let's boost Mr. James' oxygen up two liters, please and have Ariel from Respiratory come by and change his cannula."

"Got it," Chelsea said while sitting down on the chair and pulling out a hidden keyboard from underneath the desk.

She reached in her pocket, threw a few wrapped pieces of chocolates on the desk, quickly unwrapped one, and popped it into her mouth.

"You and your candy," Ronnie chuckled.

"Hey, us nurses gotta pass the time around here somehow," Chelsea replied as she began typing on the keyboard. "We ain't got it like ya'll physician assistants. Get to go all over the hospital, see a patient, and go on 'bout your business. We gotta stay, so candy it is."

Ronnie laughed. "It ain't all it's cracked up to be. We have our challenges too."

"Ain't that right, Don?"

Donald waved his hand towards his co-workers before leaning against the desk.

"And we sure have our issues," Althea said quickly, bringing herself into the conversation. She was the one and only unit secretary who handled all of the cardiac intensive care's families, patients', and medical staff's business,

Donald chuckled before lightly tapping his hand in unison with one of his favorite songs that played vividly in his mind. "Yep, I heard." *Ya'll be getting' it in anywhere and everywhere ya'll can up in here.* Donald watched as Althea

107

rummaged through the stack of folders that sat in front of her. The thoughts of Althea paraded through his mind, causing him to laugh aloud. There they were! Althea bent over, holding on to the wall in front of her, as the Chief of Cardiology, Dr. Wilder, pounded hard into her.

"What?" Althea smiled.

"Oh… Ah… Nothing," he replied. *She don't know I saw her leaning against that desk with Dr. Wilder beatin' her down.* Forcing Althea and the doctor out of his mind, his mind took its own turn and moved back into another closet. A closet and the company were both similar to Althea's scene. The difference was he saw himself, in a storage closet on the fifth floor, with Ronnie on both knees, pleasuring him like he's never been pleasured before.

"You ready?"

"Ready for…" Donald stopped as a raspy, hoarse voice stole his usual tone. Clearing his throat, he tried again. "Ready for what?"

"Me."

Donald glanced over at Althea. Althea continued to fiddle with her work, and Donald was glad. Nobody knew of his affair with Ronnie, and he worked to keep it that way. He shot Ronnie a nasty look before walking away, with Ronnie following close behind.

"So… you're just gonna act like you ain't hear what I—"

"I heard you, Ronnie. It's just…."

"Just what?"

Donald moved towards the wall as one of the floor's nurses swiftly walked by. Ronnie walked to the elevator and pressed the button marked down. Waiting for another round of people to move past, Donald nodded at the crowd before joining Ronnie. He could feel Ronnie's eyes piercing the side of his head, causing him to feel anxious. Thoughts of his pants down to his ankles and Ronnie down on the floor next to them got the best of him, bringing his manhood to full attention. Turning away, he pulled his shirt out of his pants and allowed it to fall entirely in hopes that it would cover his bulge.

"Oops, did I do that?" Ronnie purred.

Damn, Donald huffed. *Where is that damn elevator?*

"No need to hide it from me. It ain't like I ain't never seen it."

The elevator opened just as Donald reached over to slam his hand against it, allowing the pair to enter. Walking in, Donald kept as much distance as the space allowed as he saw the devilish grin etched across Ronnie's lips.

"You know you ain't gotta' deal with all the bullshit he put you through."

Donald remained quiet as the elevator slowly traveled down two floors. He forced his mind to think of something, anything, besides Ronnie's wet mouth all over his member. *Something I hate the most.* "These slow ass elevators," he said, in an attempt to change the subject to something of the complete opposite of sex and relationships. "You would think a hospital this big could afford to get the elevators fixed. All of them move too slow." Immediately, his being shifted from rock hard to a more relaxed state. Thankfully, not just mentally but physically as well.

"Nope, we not doing that."

Donald locked eyes with Ronnie and cocked his head. "Doing what?"

"Pretending that you are happy and *so* in *love*."

"I am… so—"

"That's a lie, and you know it."

Ding.

Finally! Anxious to get away from the potential danger he was in, each and every time he was alone with Ronnie, he quickly stepped off the elevator and onto the fifth floor's dimly lit and deserted hallway. He moved towards the double doors which housed most of his patients, hoping that Ronnie would join him. "Who's next?" he asked in an attempt to push the conversation into friendly territory. Seeing that his attempt was going nowhere, he tried another angle. "You ever wonder why the hospital has carpet on this floor?" A question he'd asked before but asked again, just to try to revert Ronnie's mind back to the business of taking care of patients.

"You ever think about us in the closet?"

Donald frowned. *Damn, still on it.* "You know what—?"

His body was yelling for him to engage, but his mind, well, his mind, was hard at work, working to convince his body to join it on the side of what was right. "Of course, I do…" he answered, causing his mind to lose the battle.

Following Ronnie's eyes, Donald slightly shook his head.

"No, Ronnie."

"Why not? Come on, let me make you feel good. I know you liked it the last time."

"Ronnie, I—"

"Shhh… just come on. I'll make it quick. Come on."

Again, Donald's nature began to rise. He looked over at the double doors before glancing at the infamous closet. "Ronnie, we shouldn't do that again. It was a—"

"Shhh. I know you want it. So, come on, and let's get it in real quick."

The throbbing inside his pants, coupled with the thought of Ronnie's wet mouth all over him, got the best of him. "Really quick," he whispered. Ronnie smiled and darted off to their secret sex cave. Preston was now all over, around, and in Donald's mind, but Ronnie's warm suck was calling him. Peering over at the double doors, he hurriedly walked over to the closet and closed the door behind him. Ronnie was already in position, bringing Donald to more excitement. Pulling his pants down, he shivered at the touch of Ronnie's soft hand. Leaning his back against a bundle of toilet paper packages, Donald closed his eyes and prepared for the orgasmic wave that, at this point, only Ronnie could bring. "Uhhh…" Donald moaned as Ronnie pulled him in, sucking slowly at first, then wild and erratic, just as he liked it. Donald's eyes were closed as his body burned from the tips of his toes to the crease of his upper thighs. His mind was void of all thoughts, except for the ripple that inched its way from his thighs and exploded throughout his entire body.

"Donald! Veronica?!"

Donald's eyes swung open. Ronnie hopped up, leaving Donald's hardened member fully exposed.

"What the hell is going on here?! Veronica?!"

Donald rushed to pull his pants up before saying a word to Hector, one of the hospital's beloved janitors. "We… uh…"

"You… uh…" Hector mocked. "Who does that in a storage closet? And Veronica, aren't you married?! With three kids?!"

Ronnie grabbed a scrunchie out of her lab coat pocket and pulled her thick blonde hair into a tight ball. "None of your business Hector," she mumbled.

Donald looked over at Veronica. Her cheeks were a crimson color, and the sparkle in her ocean blue eyes was now replaced with a tint of red.

"And you!"

Donald worked hard to conceal the level of embarrassment he was feeling. All he could do was stand there. Not able to defend his actions nor the actions of his friend and coworker, Ronnie's.

"Ain't you…? Never mind."

Donald dropped his head as Ronnie stormed off.

Hector sucked his teeth and walked off too, leaving Donald with his thoughts, his embarrassment, and his shame.

CHAPTER 10

I t's like he's never gonna wake up."

Preston leaned against the wall and watched as Stephanie rubbed the side of Jordan's head. Not able to say a word, he kept his eyes on anything besides the wires connected to his son.

"Come on, baby; wake up for mommy."

Preston walked over to the window and looked out into the night's sky. He smiled as his mind began to play a movie, an imaginary picture of him and Jordan, riding out on one of their father and son Sunday afternoon drives. He glanced over at Jordan and then at Stephanie. *Comfort her*, his mind roared. Moving his eyes off of Stephanie and back at the sky, he reluctantly spoke.

"Um… everything is gonna be alright."

Stephanie nodded her head. "Yeah," she sniffled.

Not sure what else to say, Preston slid his hands in his pockets and listened to Stephanie's muffled cries and the sound of the beeps of the machines.

"You know…" Stephanie began.

Damn, here she goes. Preston slightly turned away from the window, pretending to be interested in what Stephanie had to say.

"I don't even remember putting the gun in the car."

"Stephanie… not now."

"No… I'm serious, Preston." Stephanie stood up. "I don't remember putting a gun in the car. I don't even carry a gun, so how did it get in my car?"

"You know I don't know Stephanie!" Glancing over at the bed, Preston cleared his throat to lower his voice. "I don't know. Maybe one of them dudes you call *friends* put it in there."

Stephanie lowered her head, causing Preston to shake his. "When you gonna learn? Huh? When are you gonna learn that you can't have all types of men at your house, using your car and, frankly, using you?"

Stephanie kept her head lowered.

"I told you before to stay away from them dudes." Growing angrier by the second, Preston turned back towards the window. The snow glistened bushes and benches that sat in front of the window gave him a sense of peace.

"I don't know. I guess because you left and—"

"No… Nuh-uh… don't do that. Me leaving had… Listen, you ready to go yet?"

"No," Stephanie slightly shook her head. "I'm staying the night here tonight."

Preston pulled his hands out of his pockets. "Oh yeah, who's staying with you? You know you can't stay here with Jordan by yourself."

"I don't need nobody here to babysit me while I'm spending time with my son."

"Yep, you do. If it wasn't for you acting a fool the other day, then it wouldn't have to be this way."

Stephanie walked over towards the door and looked out before grabbing her purse off the bedside table. "I can call Mama."

"Nope, she isn't sufficient enough. She's just as cra…" Preston stopped himself mid-sentence before calling Janet anything besides her name. "Janet," he muttered. "She can't be here either... with you... all night.... Just the two of y'all."

"Well, how 'bout you? Why can't you—"

"Nope, I definitely can't stay with you."

"Why not? Oh, it's your *boyfriend*. What, gotta go home and be with him?"

Preston chuckled a light chuckle and leaned his left hand on the counter. "Again, Don is none of your business."

"You made him *my* business when you started messin' with him. I'm your son's mother and have the right—"

"No, you don't," Preston said as calmly as he could. "Just because we have a child together doesn't give you the right to run my life or to tell me who to have in it."

"So... You can tell me not to have people around me, but I can't tell you about the no-good people you have around you. How is that fair?"

Preston sighed loudly as he shifted his weight from his left side to his right. "Because the guys you have around you are no good, dope dealin' pimps. How do you not remember there was a gun in your car? Huh? Then you worry 'bout me and my relationship. The guys you deal with are the ones you should be worried about."

Preston shook his head as Stephanie began to cry. "Look, it's no need to continue this conversation." Standing up completely, Preston lifted his left arm and glanced at his watch. "I gotta go. Do you need a ride?"

"I told you I was staying."

"And I told you that you cannot stay here tonight. You don't have anyone to stay with you. Now, do you want me to take you home or are you going to catch a cab… the bus? What you gonna do?"

Stephanie smacked her lips and walked over to Jordan. She kissed him on the cheek, rolled her eyes at Preston, forcefully opened the sliding door, and stormed out. Preston slowly closed his eyes and quickly reopened them before following Stephanie's lead and walking over to Jordan. His eyes moved from Jordan to the breathing machine and then back at him.

"Rest, baby," he whispered as he reached down to kiss him on the forehead. Walking over to the door, he turned to look at Jordan again before walking out into the hall and closing the door behind him, leaving it ajar, just as he would if Jordan was home.

CHAPTER 11

So, what happened?"

Chad looked up from his phone and snickered. "Nothing," he answered before placing his eyes back on the social media video he'd been watching.

"Liar!" Madisyn yelped. Grabbing a throw pillow from off her bed, she playfully threw it at Chad and stood up. "You told me your dad shot his gun! So now, how is it nothing?"

Chad laughed and sat his phone on his lap. 'It was nothing. My sister came over, wanted to see her daughter. Then my moms came outside, jumped on her, and—"

"Whaattt?! For real?!"

"So, my pops came out—"

"Nah! Go back to when your mom jumped on her."

"That's it," Chad chuckled. "My moms jumped on her, they got to throwin' hands, then my pops came out and shot his gun in the air. Nothing else to tell."

Madisyn flipped over on her stomach, placed her feet on the head of the bed and snuggled them within the jumbo pillows, and focused all her attention on Chad. "What about the car?"

"Huh?"

"The car. You said on the phone that you—"

"Oh yeah, supposedly hit her with my car, but I ain't feel no bump or nothing, and ole girl ran like a bat outta hell when my pops shot his gun. So she was lying."

Madisyn nodded her head before reaching out and grabbing the throw pillow that she'd thrown at Chad and placing it under her head. Laying down, she smiled. "I guess y'all shit is way worse than ours."

"Shi… hell yeah! My sis… that girl is something serious."

"Go ahead, say it. Your sister." Madisyn giggled while lifting her legs and twisting her feet together, kicking them under the heat that blew from the vent above her bed.

"Nah, she ain't no sister of mine. My mother's daughter, yeah. But as far as *my* sister, hell naw."

"Anyway, how's—"

"Aye! Maddie?!"

Madisyn flipped herself around on the bed and hopped up. "Yeah?!"

"Girl! Come with me to my house and help me…. Oh, I ain't know Chad was here."

"Hey, Chad."

"How you doing, Deborah?"

"Good."

"What's wrong?" Madisyn frowned.

"Girl, my husband… your brother… is trippin'. He talkin' bout going over to Preston's house and smacking his boyfriend."

"What? Why?"

"Girl, something bout he heard Donald talkin' bout something about Jordan and—"

"Jordan?"

"Yeah, he didn't give me no details," Deborah slowly shrugged her shoulders.

Glancing over at Chad, Chad followed Deborah's lead and shrugged his shoulders before hopping up and grabbing his coat. Sliding on her sneakers, Madisyn quickly tied the left strings before pulling her coat off the chair that sat in the corner of the room.

"What did he say?"

"Girl, I done told you... I don't know." Deborah walked out into the hallway and folded her arms. "Just come on so we can see wassup."

Madisyn looked over at Chad while zipping her coat.

CHAPTER 12

*T*wenty-five thousand, two hundred, sixty-two dollars, and fourteen cents. Donald glared at his computer. "My life savings. I can't give her none of this money, even if it won't dent it too much. I worked too hard for this savings." Looking up at the clock, he pushed his laptop slightly to his right and laid his head on the kitchen table. His mind reverted back to yet another phone call from Heather and the argument she'd continued to provoke.

Pay me my money... pay me my money, he heard Heather's voice yelling at him. Twisting his head from his right to his left, he moved from one disaster to another. The memory of him and Ronnie getting caught in their secret spot. *Damn,* he mumbled before turning again to his right side. Heather reemerged. Her voice was full of anger as she demanded to be paid for the job, or she would expose the secret and reveal her truth. Sighing, he turned his head back to his left, and again, there was Ronnie. On her knees, causing his body to scream out in ecstasy. Flipping his head back to his right, he saw Heather staring at him as if he were the devil himself.

"Damn!" He shouted before lifting his head off the table. "It's like I'm in the damn twilight zone." Standing, he gazed at the computer screen and folded his arms. "I guess I could start over with my savings. But then, what about Preston? How would I explain withdrawing any amount of the money when we're both supposed to be saving?" The harsh wind blared from the outside, signaling that Channel Ten's Evening News was, in fact, correct to forecast the first major snowstorm of the year was on its way. Focusing on the blustery wind and the sound of the shutters beating against the house, he walked into the living room and flopped down on the couch. He listened as the storm strengthened, adding sleet to the mix. "Ronnie, what the hell was I thinking? Well, I'm sure Preston's been cheating on me… probably for years."

What proof do you have? Did you actually find anything? Have you ever seen him with anyone else? His mind sneered at him, bringing him yet again to another argument within himself.

"Yeah," he answered, determined to not allow his subconscious state to win the battle against his conscious mind. "That time, he consoled his baby mama after she beat my ass. And on my own porch…by the way!" His conscious mind yelled.

Ok, but who did he go to the hospital with? Didn't she go off to jail after that? His subconscious mind spat back.

Donald leaned his head against the arm of the couch. Not wanting to admit the fact that his subconscious thoughts were indeed winning the argument.

"The way he looked at her, though. If I wasn't standing there, the fool would've gone off with her to make sure she was straight," his conscious mind tried once more to finally overpower and win.

But he didn't. That's the key point here, Don. He didn't!

"Yeah, well…" the storm door opened, followed by the sound of keys entering the door's lock. Donald sat up straight, mentally forcing his mind to hush, ending the argument.

"Hey," he said calmly as Preston rushed in.

Preston slightly jumped. "Whoa, wasn't expecting you to be sitting in here in the dark. Wassup?"

Donald squinted his eyes and nodded his head as Preston flipped the light on and slammed the door shut.

"Just chillin', long day today." Thinking of conversation, Donald watched as Preston slid out of his coat and kicked his boots off at the door. "Um… so, how's the lil man doing?" Adding a smile for emphasis, he repositioned himself on the couch.

Preston sighed loudly and flopped down in the recliner. "I don't really know."

Donald frowned. Guilt ripped into him like tiny knives cutting slowly into his skin, shredding it into tiny pieces.

"He's just laying there, still on all those machines and stuff. We just don't know if he…."

Donald dropped his head at the sound of Preston's cracking voice.

"He… um…"

"Hey… it's okay. Let's just talk about something else."

Preston nodded.

Both Ronnie and Heather stood tall in his mind, reminding him of his dirty deed with one situation and scandalous lie with the other. Shaking them away, he stood up. "How's your mom feeling?" *Oh, way to go, Donald. You ask about one sick family member to another who's sick. Way... to... go!*

"Yeah, Mama, she's good. Preston rubbed his right hand over the top of his head. "I need to get over there and see her. Hopefully tomorrow."

Donald titled his head and smiled, grateful that his question didn't sour Preston's mood further. "That's good. Hey... maybe I can go over there with you."

Preston lifted his feet in the recliner and chuckled. "Yeah."

A chuckle. What's that all about. "Yeah?" Donald repeated. Walking into the kitchen, he looked up at the clock. *Ten fifty-two.* Glancing back in the living room, he bit down on his lower lip, not sure what else to chat about. Trying his hardest to think of something festive to talk about, he came up with nothing. His mind was full but not from anything he could freely share. So, he resorted back to what both he and Preston always did when the air was thick of uncertainty or anger, finding an excuse to leave. "I'm going to take a

129

shower." He waited for a response but was only greeted with the roar of the wind and smack of the sleet against the windows. "Uh... I'm going to—"

"I heard you, Don."

Lightly smacking his lips, he waved his right hand and looked over at the laptop. Then back towards the living room, and then back at his laptop. The multicolored squiggly lines replaced the bank statement that held the key to burying his secret. Heather's frown removed his attention from Preston's attitude, bringing him to unrest that he had no idea how to cure. Closing the laptop, he grabbed it and walked into the bedroom. Placing it on the bed, he removed his shirt and tossed it into the hamper before going into the bathroom. Hoping that a nice, hot shower would temporarily wash away his indiscretions.

"It was your idea, Deborah."

"Yeah, but how was I supposed to know that it was gonna be a storm tonight."

"It's called the news! You know when the meteorologist stands at the screen with a stick in hand?!" Madisyn yelled.

"Ya'll chill," Chad said calmly. *Out of all the places for you to stall, you had to choose Monroe and Benson. Where all the junkies be at. Beggin' and shit.*

"And why is it that you don't have a car that can handle snow? How long you been living here?"

Chad shifted his eyes towards Deborah and opened his mouth to clap back, but his father's voice boomed. *Just shut up and let 'em talk, Son.*

The wind blew hard, lightly shaking the stranded car. "Well, at least we are close to my parents' house. We can walk over there."

"Huh? Don't your parents stay on Obama Lane?"

"Yeah."

"Chadbert, that's not right down the street. That's like a mile from here, and I ain't walking out in that!" Madisyn said as she swung her right hand towards the windshield.

"Not Chadbert," Deborah chortled.

The car grew silent. Madisyn, in the passenger seat, with a deep frown on her face. Deborah sat directly behind Madisyn with her face glued to the window, watching the storm. Chad sat in his seat, embarrassed that his car suffered another breakdown. Unfortunately, this time it was in front of his girlfriend and her chatty sister-in-law. This woman was known to make fun of someone else's misfortunes for weeks and sometimes even years. Unlocking his phone, he tapped his mother's number and listened to the ringing, hoping that it wouldn't go to voicemail. *Come on, Ma*, he mumbled just as the ringing paused, giving way to the voicemail. Hanging up, he glanced over at Madisyn before fixing his eyes on the huge orbs of snow. Pushing his mother's contact again, he listened to the ringing phone until voice mail again answered on her behalf.

"Can't you turn on the heat or something?" Deborah asked loudly as she folded both arms and began to rub her arms. "It's cold."

Chad kept his eyes on the snow, not bothering to answer.

"Girl, the car is dead. That means the heat is too." Madisyn answered for Chad.

Deborah smacked her lips. "Well, let me use your phone."

"I left it at the house."

Deborah sighed and turned her attention to Chad. "Let me use yours?"

Chad lightly sucked his teeth. "Where's yours?"

"Dead!" Deborah yelled.

"Girl, chill out and lower your voice. You ain't gotta do all that."

"Then don't ask stupid questions. I mean… why would I ask to borrow yours if mine was working?"

"Whateva," Chad said before dropping his phone down on his lap

"Chad?!" Madisyn quipped.

"What?"

"You not gonna let her use your phone?"

Chad sighed before picking his phone up and handing it to Deborah.

"Gee… thanks. It's a shame your girlfriend had to tell you what to do."

"Deb."

Deborah ignored Madisyn's plea and continued to nag at Chad. "What? I wouldn't even need to use his phone if his car didn't break down. Got us out here in a damn snowstorm."

"And if it wasn't for you and your bright idea to find your husband so he wouldn't confront Donald about some shit that's none of my business or yours, then we wouldn't even be out here!"

"Chad!"

"Madisyn, you know I'm right. Why are we even going over to your brother's house to ask his man about what he got going on? Oh, wait, what *her* husband says Donald got going on. Donald ain't never done nothing to me... to none of us. So why are we going over there and...?" Chad squinted his eyes and sat up straight.

"What?"

"Wow." Chad glanced over his left shoulder to see Deborah tapping his phone. "Who you tryin' to call? Your husband?"

Deborah sighed and continued to punch numbers into Chad's phone.

"All you gotta do is go across the street."

Both Deborah and Madisyn looked up to follow Chad's eyes. Two men stood in front of the corner store; one was wiping his nose while the other was sniffing.

"Aw hell naw," Deborah muttered.

"I thought he was done with that stuff," Madisyn whispered.

"Apparently not," Chad chuckled.

Deborah sucked her teeth before sighing loudly and opening the door.

"Uh-uh, you ain't going over there."

Deborah ignored Madisyn, stepped her left foot out into the soft, slippery snow, followed by her right, and slammed the car door. Madisyn pulled the handle to open the passenger door.

"Aye, you stay here!"

"I can't let her go over there and start acting a fool! She got kids at home!"

"And? Listen, I know he's your brother, and she's your sister-in-law… your girl and all… but you ain't got nothing to do with what they got going on." Chad pushed his

135

seat back and grabbed his phone off the back seat. Typing in his password, he opened his calls list and tapped his mother's name. He kept his eyes on Deborah as she stormed over to her husband, slipping twice before she made it over to him.

"Why did you have to say anything anyways?" Madisyn snarled.

Chad waited until he heard his mother's voice mail greeting before he answered. Pushing the end button, he leaned his head back and looked over at Madisyn. "She was gonna see him anyway. If I noticed him, I know good and well she would... eventually. Ain't no need to keep calling him if he's right over there."

Madisyn put her head in her hands. "He promised Daddy before he died that he was done with all that. I can't believe he's back at it."

"Hmmm... maybe he ain't ever stop."

Madisyn looked over at Chad with fury in her eyes.

"I'm sorry, baby but some junk...."

Madisyn opened her mouth and angrily twisted her body towards Chad.

"People…" Chad corrected before Madisyn had the chance to verbally cut him. "With bad habits, never really learn."

"Well…" Madisyn started.

Yoooo, Chad mumbled.

They both watched in silence as Deborah was knocked to the ground. Madisyn reached for the door again, and again, Chad stopped her. "No, leave it alone."

"He just hit her!"

"Yeah, and if you go over there, he might hit you too, and then I'd have to jump in it. You know your brother loses his mind when he's on that shit. I don't even know why she went over there."

Chad's phone vibrated, and his mother's face illuminated on the screen. "Finally," he said before answering.

"Hey, Ma! Can you come get me?" He nodded his head at Madisyn before glancing back at the fight that was taking place between Deborah and Leon. Deborah was now back on her feet, punching a stoned-out Leon as he continued his business of getting high. "Yeah, we on Monroe street. Across from… Long story Ma. I'll tell you all about it when you get here… Alright… Okay, Ma." Clicking the phone off, he shook his head at the fiasco taking place and closed his eyes at the side-eye he was receiving from an angry Madisyn.

CHAPTER 13

Stephanie laid down across her bed as she stared out into the snow. She looked down at the picture of Jordan before repositioning herself on the bed. The one and only streetlight on the street shined brightly in the night's sky, shedding light on the snow that fell lightly. She tried her hardest to think of something, anything, besides her baby. Still, her mind had its way, bringing nothing to it but Jordan and his injured, unconscious body. Sitting up, she pulled the king-sized pillow from the top of the bed. She placed it under her head before closing her eyes, hoping that she would finally get sleepy enough to actually fall asleep.

"Yes, come on in." Her mom's voice traveled through Stephanie's closed bedroom door.

Popping her eyes open, Stephanie sat up and trotted over to the door.

"She should be in here somewhere."

Mama, damn it.

"Stephanie?! Come on out here."

Bubbling anger began to burn within the pit of Stephanie's stomach. She leaned her body against the wall and counted to ten before forcing her mouth into a smile.

"Steph?!"

Sighing under her breath, she glanced over at Jordan's picture on the bed, using it to gather the strength and power needed to have a conversation with her mother. Breathing a quick breath, she smoothed her hair down and walked towards the living room.

"Hey Ma, I was just…" she frowned at her mother's companion before placing her eyes on her. "Ma? What is he doing here?"

"Well, love, he came to check up on Jordan."

Stephanie stood in the middle of her living room, feeling both dazed and nauseous. The one man who she hated most was standing there, in her home, and her mother was the one to bring him to her. Her inner voice whispered to her to defend herself and her house, but she was stuck. Stuck at the fact that James Bradley was in her presence, smiling as if he didn't do the ungodly and filthy things he'd done. As if he had not spiked her drink with some sort of drug to have her out of her mind. As if he had not taken her clothes off and violated her, spreading his DNA all in, around, and over her, creating her one and only pregnancy. As if he'd forgotten that he was her uncle, and she was his little sister's daughter!

"No, uh-uh, Mama! He is not supposed to be here!"

"Relax! Sit down!"

Stephanie looked her uncle up and down before following her mother's orders and throwing herself down on the couch.

"Now I know ya'll have had some issues, but—"

"Issues?! Mama, he–he rap—!"

"Uh… No ma'am. We are not going there again."

Stephanie glared at her uncle before sliding herself back into the couch. *I cannot believe that man is here right now.*

"Now, is there a list or something of people that can go up and see him? If so, you need to call the hospital and get him on the list."

Stephanie rolled her eyes and moved closer to the furthest end of the couch. The sight of him made her want to find some source of shelter, some source of protection, as her mother never offered any. Hugging herself, she kept her eyes on the hand-painted portrait of an aqua blue ocean accompanied by a breathtaking sunset that sat on the wall in front of her. She decided to use her surroundings to drown out the hatred she felt for her uncle and the disappointment she held for his sister. *Just imagine you're there, Stephanie. There on the beach, watching the sunset.*

"Aye!"

"Huh?"

"You haven't heard a word I said."

Blankly staring at her mother, Stephanie waited for her to continue with whatever she was saying.

"Now call him."

"Um…?"

"Preston. Call him and let him know that we are all here, and he needs to hurry up."

A rush of emotions flooded Stephanie, causing the nausea she was feeling to increase by twenty. "What?" she asked in a hushed, raspy whisper.

"You heard me. It's time for Preston to know the truth. In case…"

Stephanie kept her eyes on her mother, not believing any of the words that she was speaking.

"Listen, baby. We just don't know how things will turn out. I think it's best if Jordan's father gets the chance to spend…" Janet smiled, abandoning the rest of her sentence.

Stephanie swallowed hard as the urge to vomit was at its strongest. The bright lights pierced through the sheer curtains and added extra light to the living room's dim lighting. Stephanie looked towards the window and back at her mother. Reading her mind, Janet answered her daughter's question. "Oh, I called him already. Told him to meet me over here."

"Then why did you just tell me to call him?!" Stephanie yelled, suddenly finding the umph and strength needed to finally stand up to her mother.

James snickered and sat down on the chair that sat behind him.

"Did I tell you that you could have a seat in my house?!"

"Stephanie, don't be rude and fix your tone when you speakin' to me."

Stephanie used every ounce of strength in her not to go off on her mother or her uncle. She was just about ready to explode, both mentally and physically. The living room's light was now back to its weakened state as the lights from a pair of car's headlights were shut off. Rushing to the window, she looked out to see the driver's side of Preston's car door open. Feeling short of breath, she fumbled with her mind to produce calming thoughts but unlucky for her, her mind was in full-fledged panic mode.

"You want me to go—" her mother offered.

"No! I got it."

Breathing in deeply and exhaling slowly, Stephanie walked over to the door, quickly opened it, and stepped out onto the porch, being sure to slam the door behind her.

"What's this all about? What's going on?"

Stephanie stood frozen solid, like a deer caught in headlights on a dark country road.

"What is your mother calling me for?"

"Uh," Stephanie uttered just as the door opened behind her. Startled, she turned to see her mother's smiling face as she joined her on the porch.

"Ohhh, it's cold out here. Preston! Thank you for coming."

Snow began to fall heavier as Preston made his way up to the porch. "What is it?" He asked impatiently while pulling his hood over his head.

"Come on in, and I'll show you," Janet answered. Smiling at her daughter, she snatched the door open and disappeared behind it. As Preston followed, Stephanie watched helplessly, leaving her on the porch with her fears, frustrations, and torment.

Rubbing the towel over his legs, Donald stopped and looked in the mirror. The facial hair on his face was at the longest it's ever been, which bothered him. "I gotta get myself back in order. Might be why my man ain't tryin' to...."

CRASH!

"What the hell?!" Coming out of the bathroom, Donald moved through his bedroom and peeped out into the hallway.

"Preston?!"

Stepping his right foot out into the hall, he peeped his head out further. "Preston?!" He called out a bit louder. Going back into the bedroom, he threw the towel on the floor and grabbed a pair of black basketball shorts off the chair, and slipped them on. He then walked back to the door and called out again. "Aye! Preston, is that you?" He was greeted by the sound of silence, followed by another startling crash. Startled, he jumped backward and stood behind the door. *Fight or Flight* moment. *Flight!* His mind answered for him. *Uh-uh, this my house*, he breathed. *I'd rather fight.* His eyes darted around the room until they landed on Jordan's starter baseball bat that was conveniently sitting in the corner. *Lil man's bat.* Grabbing it, he sighed at the miniature bat before refocusing his attention on the task at hand. *Better than nothing.* Taking one final deep breath, he lifted the bat and charged out of his bedroom, into the hallway, and out into the living room. The curtains that once hung neatly at the bay windows were now in company with the snow as the wind held both of them, hostage, flinging them around in its strength. He lowered the bat at the sight of shattered glass on the floor with a brown brick lying on top of it.

"Shit!" Tossing the bat on the couch, he moved closer to the mess, bent over to get a closer look at the brick, and yelled out again. "Damn it!" He hollered before storming out of the living room and back to his bedroom. Slipping his feet in his slippers, anger gripped him as he forcefully pulled open his drawer and snatched a long-sleeved shirt out, not worrying about reclosing the drawer. "No need to try to figure out who did this shit!" Heather danced viciously in his mind while he pulled the shirt over his head and made his way back into the living room.

I don't even know if I should call the police. What would I tell them? "Hey Officer, my crazy ass stepdaughter threw a brick in my house. Then his ass gonna want to know why. My answer… because I wouldn't pay her for shooting my stepson. Now, Officer, I didn't pay her because she was supposed to shoot my stepson's mother! Not the child! Ha, picture that shit!"

The faint buzz of the heater popped on, replacing some of the noise that the wind was making. The snow was falling hard, some into the hole that was once his spring-cleaning project; his beautiful windows he picked out and put up himself. One job that he was immensely proud of. "Ugh!" He surveyed the rest of the room. To his surprise, everything else was intact. "How the hell will I get this covered? Ain't nothing in…" he stopped himself as thoughts of Preston joined Heather. Both staring him down with hatred in their eyes. "How the hell will I explain this to Preston?"

He walked into the kitchen, picked up the broom in his left hand and the dustpan in the other, and threw them both in the living room. Stomach pains from his untreated gastric ulcer were beginning to form, but he ignored them. Instead of thinking of the ulcer that acted up only when he was in severe stress, he leaned against the counter in full clean-up mode. He didn't know where Preston was, but he knew that he would be home soon, and before Preston walked through the door, he had to have his lies straight and his game tight.

He turned to see Stephanie slowly walking in the door before planting his eyes on a wickedly smiling Janet and a man he had never met before.

"Thank you for coming, Preston. We—"

"What do you want, Janet? Stephanie?"

Stephanie put her head down and leaned her hips against the fireplace mantle. Preston glanced over at her and shook his head before turning to Janet.

"Well, had you let me finish… you could've already known why you're here."

Itching to speak, with added cussing, Preston fought his urge and remained silent. Wishing that he were anywhere besides standing in front of who he deemed the most dysfunctional people he's ever met.

"So… I invited you here to meet James."

Preston turned towards James and nodded his head. "How you doing?"

"I'm doing fine young man, just fine."

Preston slowly turned back towards Janet. "Listen, Janet, I need to—"

"Go and see Jordan?"

"Among other things, yes. So… it was nice talking to you."

"Um…?"

"James."

"Yeah, James, it was a pleasure meeting you. Stephanie, I'll talk to you later."

Preston turned away from the crowd and waved before making it to the door. *Crazy ass people.* Turning the knob, he opened the screen door and stepped his right foot onto the porch.

"Why don't you take Jordan's father with you? He's excited to finally meet him. Right, James?" Janet sneered.

The feeling of being punched in the gut was an understatement compared to how Preston was feeling. His chest was on fire, and his mind was in shambles.

"He doesn't drive… Eyes ain't what they used to be, so we were hoping you would take him over there." Janet continued with her evil revelation.

Preston kept his body on the porch, not wanting to deal with any more of Janet or claiming that James was his son's father. Balling his lips, he moved his foot back into the house. *May as well deal with this bitch and her crazy antics now.* "Janet, it's late. I'm tired. And I don't have time for your bullshit right now."

"Bullshit?" Janet said through a hate-filled laugh.

"Stephanie, go on, tell him. Let that man know the real truth, so he can go and live the life he wants to live. With his man and with no strings attached."

Preston sighed and shook his head. "Stephanie, I gotta go. I'll talk to you later."

Stephanie looked over at her mother and then back at Preston. "Yeah," she mumbled.

Preston frowned. "Yeah, what?!"

"It's true! Okay?!" Stephanie screamed.

Preston stared at Stephanie as if she had just landed on Earth from some mythical, fairytale kingdom and was there to take him back home with her.

"I-I was raped and—"

"Stop!" Preston put his left hand up. "Just stop. Now, I'ma go before I start handing out ass whippings up in here." Storming to the door, Preston wasted no time walking out and slamming the door behind him.

"Preston! Wait!"

Ignoring Stephanie, Preston rushed to his car, slammed his finger on the unlock button on his key fob, forcefully snatched the door open, and hopped in. Janet's words and James' smile burned into his mind, giving him an excruciating headache.

"Preston!"

Ignoring Stephanie, he turned the ignition, clicked on the headlights, and snapped the car into reverse. Taking one final look at Stephanie, his heart sank from the devastating betrayal and the look of hurt and sadness on her face. *Maybe the ole bitch is lying.* He used his headlights to take a good look at Stephanie. Her eyes were full of not only tears but pain that he had never seen before. Putting the car back in park, he left the car running as he opened the door and hopped back out. *Something's not right.* He thought as his gut was engulfed with a wildfire. But this time, it wasn't just the anger and rage of Janet's words but something about Stephanie's look. "So, it's true?" He stammered.

Stephanie was now crying uncontrollably, which gave him his answer.

"Noooo… Oh my God!" he mumbled. A few drops of sleet fell lightly from the sky, hitting him on the face. "Stephanie? Why?"

"Yes… Okay… I got pregnant… after he…."

Preston kept his eyes on Stephanie as she explained through muffled tears.

"He raped me. My uncle—"

"Your uncle?!" Preston just could not believe what he was hearing.

Stephanie nodded her head.

The sleet began to fall heavier now. Preston moved backward, all the while, keeping his eyes on Stephanie.

"He raped me, Preston."

Turning, he trotted to his car. His head was now in tune with his stomach, both aching and burning. His thoughts were all over the place, from storming off and leaving town, leaving everything and everybody to forcing his way back into Stephanie's house and knocking people out. The latter won. His boots hit heavily on the sidewalk as he ran in lighting speed towards Stephanie. Brushing past her, he heard her screams and yells but ignored them.

Opening the screen door, he forced his way in, intentionally walking as close as he could to Janet and nudging her before making his way to his target. **POW!** He punched James hard in the eye, causing him to fall to the floor.

"Preston! No!" Stephanie cried.

"Are you crazy?!" Janet followed while she dropped to her knees to comfort her brother.

"Yeah, bitch! I am, and now you can finally see for yourself!"

"James! Come on, James. Wake up!" Janet pleaded.

Getting in a glance, Preston saw that James was knocked out cold. Which, in turn, alleviated some of the burning anger that had his stomach in knots.

"Oh, no! He's not breathing. Call the ambulance, Stephanie! Your uncle is not breathing!"

Stephanie stood paralyzed, not able to move a muscle.

"James! Come on, James! Get up! You killed him!" Janet yelled. "You son of a bitch! You killed my brother!"

CHAPTER 14

"Get yo' stupid ass up!"

Heather gathered herself and rubbed a spot of blood off her mouth. The swelling surrounding her left eye throbbed as her right cheek burned from the gash placed there a few seconds after Silk rushed in. He demanded to know why his daughter was gone and why there was still no money for him to buy more product.

"You still ain't get no money from that fool yet?! Damn! How long is it goin' to take you to get it?!"

Heather lifted herself off the floor and dropped down on the bed. Her body felt heavy, heavy like a sac of potatoes that had just been picked. Her face looked like she'd spent some time in the ring with Floyd Mayweather after he'd won one of his knockout boxing matches.

"And how you gonna let yo' mama take my daughter?! I told you before to stop letting her just come in and take her!"

Heather opened her mouth to speak but was silenced by the sting that the movement produced. Her body ached, and her mind screamed. *If you were around to help me, maybe my mama wouldn't have to come and get her.*

"What the hell is taking you so long to get the money?!"

Moving her mouth, Heather winced as the pain grabbed her. "I..." stopping to gather her strength, she moved her mouth around in small circles before trying to speak out. "I have to..." her eyes watered with tears as she struggled to make a complete full sentence. "Wait," she said quickly.

"That's the problem, Stupid! We don't have time to wait! I got to catch Twin before he leave!"

YOU gotta catch him... not me, so not my problem.

"Plus, I gotta pay him back for the shit you smoked. Damn, Heather, you can't do shit right!"

Heather watched helplessly as Silk circled around her. She hoped he'd gotten his satisfaction for the day and move along out into the street. Or over to his other baby's mother's house but to her dismay, he sat down beside her. She tried everything in her power to not react, but his presence always made her jumpy.

"Look, I'm sorry for… It's just that I got a lot going on, and we need that money." Silk placed his arm on Heather's right thigh, and she jumped. "Not only for us but for Ashanti too."

The smell of him made Heather's stomach hurt. A fragrance that she once loved was now the worst. Anytime she smelled that smell, it meant a beating for her.

"Um…" she started.

"Let's go over there; maybe I can get him to give us the money." Silk suggested.

Heather slowly shook her head.

"What?" Silk stood, instantly intensifying the fear.

"I mean… not right now." That one statement could cost her five straight minutes of throbbing pain, but she'd deal with it if it meant convincing Silk not to go over to Donald's house and possibly beating him down. Although she didn't show it, she still considered Donald as her father. The only person who really cared about her besides her biological father.

"Girl, get your shit together and come on. Ain't nobody playin' wit' you!"

Standing, Heather picked up an old towel from off the floor and walked into the bathroom. She gasped at the sight the cracked mirror reflected. Her brown eyes were now enveloped in huge dark circles, and her once full, puckered lips were swollen on the left side and dented on the right. Pulling her hair back, she leaned down and grabbed one of the ponytail holders that was knocked to the floor during the beating. Nervously, she tied her long curly hair up in it before turning the hot water on. She glared at her face in the mirror while waiting for the water to heat up.

"Aye!"

Startled, she dropped the towel before leaning both hands on the sink.

"Hurry up!"

She lowered her head and balled her fist. "Why do I keep putting up with him?" Bending down, she kept her left hand on the sink while using her right hand to retrieve the towel. Throwing the top half into the sink, she frowned while drenching the towel in the water, wrung it out, and began cleaning the mess that her abuser spread all over her face.

"What the hell is this?!"

Donald jumped up off the bed and rushed into the living room. Seeing the look of both shock and anger on Preston's face, he began with his rehearsed excuse. "I don't know what the hell happened. I guess somebody tried to break in."

"Break in?! Preston shrieked. "Why the hell would somebody break this big ass window to break in?"

Good question; I wasn't counting on that one. Donald quipped internally. He worked hard to contain his mind but was having no luck at all with the task. "Um, I guess—"

"Donald, what is going on? Be real with me. What's the problem? You been acting weird ever since—"

"It's you."

"Me?" Preston asked while eyeing the sheet-covered window and slowly evaluating the damages. "What about me? The fact that I have a son…" he stopped himself at the sight of Stephanie, her mother, and her rapist uncle.

"Preston, I—"

"Just save it, Donald. I can't do this right now. I guess we'll wait until the police get here." *Oh shit, the police.* His mind reverted back to the solid punch to the face he gave James just over an hour ago.

Donald watched quietly as Preston slowly walked past him.

"You did call the police… right?" He asked only for the sake of chastising Donald as he was not ready to deal with any kind of law enforcement, especially not the police officers from the local precinct.

"Uh… Nah, not yet. I wanted to cover it first before I called. You know, to keep as much snow out as I can."

Preston looked over at the window. "Well, that ain't working," he pointed. "You might wanna—"

BOOM! BOOM! BOOM!

Both Donald and Preston stopped in their tracks. Preston's heart began to beat ten times harder than the regular rate, and Donald was just about ready to faint.

DING DONG! DINGGGGG DONG!

"Yo, who is that trying to get in so bad?!" Annoyed, Preston didn't wait for an answer from Donald. He marched to the door and quickly opened it.

"Can I help you?"

"You Donald?"

Preston turned to look at Donald and then back at their guest. "And you are?"

"I'm the man who's gonna beat his ass! Now, are you him?!"

Preston sarcastically laughed before planting his eyes on the man's companion, the woman standing out in the snow.

"Uh, ma'am, you don't have to stand out there. Come on up here."

"Don't say nothing to…" the man huffed loudly before he continued. "Is your name Donald?! That's all I wanna know! We can skip all the nice shit!"

"Man, who are *you*?!" Now, Preston was agitated with the raging bull standing at his door.

Donald sighed and walked over to the door, slightly moving Preston off to the side.

161

"Donald, what the hell is…? What the…?"

The irate stranger didn't say another word before he punched Donald, sending him to his knees.

Glancing over at Donald, Preston rushed the guy, both of them falling on the porch. Adrenaline grabbed Donald, giving him the boost needed to pull Preston off the man.

"Stop!" The woman yelled as she inched her way backward and away from the commotion. Lacking both time and energy to deal with the woman who was yelling in the background, Donald continued his quest to stop the two men from pounding into each other. Preston got one last strike in before Donald lifted him completely off his opponent. Rushing Preston through what was left of their storm door, Donald looked into the face of a monster.

"Aye! The next time you want your dick sucked, it better not come from my wife's mouth! Stay the fuck away from her!" The man jogged down the steps, snatched his companion's hand, and forcefully stormed his way out the yard and into the darkness. Just as quick as he'd arrived, he was gone.

"You alright?" Donald tenderly placed his right hand on Preston's back.

"Let me go!" Preston yelled before walking back into the house.

Donald took a glance into the yard and surveyed what the streetlights would allow him to see of the neighborhood before joining Preston. *Ronnie! Why the hell did she tell her husband?! Why would she bring him to my house?!* He tugged at the storm door but had no luck pulling it closed completely due to the broken hinge, so he left it and closed the exterior door, making sure to snap the lock in place. *The next time you want your dick sucked...* Ronnie's husband's words stung Donald's mind. *Maybe Preston didn't understand, or maybe... didn't hear what the guy said. Maybe because they'd just got finished fighting, he—*

"So, you got your dick sucked, huh?!"

All thoughts were now as quiet as a mouse running around a dark kitchen.

"You out here... getting your dick sucked... by some married woman... when my son is in the hospital... fighting for his fuckin' life!" Preston was still out of breath from the fight; however, he was still ready for Round Two with Donald.

Donald was frozen solid, not sure what to say. *Say something! Maybe start with… it wasn't me!* "I don't—"

"Stop! Don't do that. All that it wasn't me or you don't know what he talkin' bout. I don't want to hear none of that bull!"

Donald kept quiet. The burn and pain in Preston's voice bothered him, but he had no idea how to extinguish it.

"Just man up!" Preston stood up and walked towards the bedroom. "Just be a man about it all. If you wanted to get it sucked, then just say I wanted it sucked. Not hard to do."

Wind gust burst through the sheet that hung in front of the window. Another round of sleet began falling, not giving Baltimoreans much of a break from the risk of slipping and falling. It fell heavily, causing some of it to seep through the sheet, shoot past the window's protrusion and drop onto the floor. Watching as the bands of sleet fell through, Donald couldn't focus on the mess that was being made in his living room. Not just the sleet's mess but his own mess wasn't an option to deal with at this point as he just didn't know how. Now knowing what to say or what to do, he sat down on the arm of the chair and put his head into his hands. Chirping from a distance joined the noise of the occasional sleet that fell to the floor. Lifting his head, he readjusted his feet and peered towards the bedroom. The door was closed. He looked down at the bottom of the door to see that the light was off. Another chirp rang out.

Checking his immediate surroundings, he felt around in the chair before looking towards the kitchen. Standing, he made his way through the living room, past the bedroom, and into the kitchen. His phone sat on the table, displaying a new message. He glared at the unfamiliar number to which the text was sent before he grabbed his phone and read silently.

Next time… it be yo head I smash… not the window. The next time you fuck wit my wife.

Slamming the phone down, he leaned his hand against the wall and fixed his eyes on the window. A good mixture of both snow and sleet rushed in with a gust of wind. *The last time I trust some bitch at work,* he mumbled before grabbing the mop and walking back into the living room.

CHAPTER 15

Y ou said he did what?!"

"Yep, I saw him, Mama, with my own eyes."
Madisyn pulled another roller out of her
mother's hair as she explained the fight between her brother
and his wife.

"Lord, I was praying that he was done with that mess.
One of your daddy's dying wishes."

"Yeah," Madisyn nodded her head. "I was hoping
Leon would finally get himself together… for good this
time."

"Me too, baby."

Madisyn continued to unroll her mother's hair, all the
while thinking of the fiascos that happened during her stint
in Chad's cold, broken-down car.

"I guess we just gotta keep—"

"Hey, Ma."

Annie looked up to see Preston standing in the
kitchen's doorway.

"Hey, baby! What in the world? W-What happened?"

Madisyn frowned at the small cut above her brother's left eye. "Don't tell me Donald's into giving black eyes now."

Preston sighed and sat down across from Annie. "It's nothing. Just a misunderstanding."

"A misunderstanding? What does that mean?"

"Mama, you are a retired teacher; you know what that means."

Madisyn cut her eyes over at Preston while grabbing the rat tail comb off the table.

"Don't you sass me, Preston Alligood Dixon!"

Preston nodded his head before lowering it. "I'm sorry, Ma, just going through a lot."

All voices were now quiet, allowing the gospel song playing low on the radio to serenade the Dixon house.

Call on Jesus, Annie sang in tune with the song.

Madisyn glanced over at Preston while he kept his head down. "So... you wanna tell us what happened?" She asked as she pulled the last roller out, opened the hair conditioner, and smoothed a little on her finger. She looked over at Preston while she tilted her mother's head and parted a small portion of her hair before spreading some of the conditioner onto her scalp.

"Nothing," Preston said quickly. "Just a—"

"Chile!"

All eyes refocused all attention at the front of the house.

"I knew that man wasn't no good! Out here messin' with coworkers and..." Deb stopped and gasped when she saw Preston and the frown that was strong on his face.

"Ain't you supposed to be in jail?" Preston asked as he angrily stood up and wiped his right hand on the top of his head.

"Hey, Preston. Nah, I got out the other day. Thanks to my auntie."

Annie smiled and nodded her head. "You're welcome, baby."

"Mama!"

Annie, Deborah, and Madisyn all turned to wait for Preston to finish whatever he planned to say.

"What?"

"You... where'd you get money to bail her out? Please don't tell me you used Daddy's money?"

Madisyn sucked her teeth while parting another area of Annie's hair and saturating it with the cream.

"So, what if I did? Your daddy didn't tell me what I could and couldn't do with the money he left for *me*."

"And... Deb went to jail for fighting yo' baby mama," Madisyn added.

Preston shook his head before walking out of the kitchen and into the hallway. He rubbed his temples while looking at his father's picture. His eyes danced around from one family photo to another, stopping at a smiling Jordan. *Damn.* Walking into the living room, he dropped down on the couch and leaned his head on the back of the cushion. Deb's voice was louder than loud in his mind as he watched the replay of her walking into the house with some juicy details about someone else's life. *What was she getting ready to say?* He switched his head from his right to his left. *Why did she stop when she saw me? She ain't never finish what she started.* Laughter came from the kitchen, bringing him to a tremendous feeling of unease. *What the hell is so funny?*

170

"It's a complete mess, Chile!" Deb's voice boomed through the house.

Preston lifted his head and stood up. The memory of his fight with Stephanie's uncle and the scuffle he had with some man who claimed his wife had some type of entanglement with Donald were the topics that had his mind on fire. Moreover, Deb's laughter and comments were doing nothing to help extinguish it.

"Whew! I'm tellin' ya'll."

Preston leaned forward on the couch at the sound of Deb's laughter and heavy footsteps coming closer towards the living room.

"How you doing, Cuz?"

Preston looked at Deb, trying to complete the impossible and get a glimpse into her brain to invade her thoughts.

"What? You alright?"

Looking past her and towards the kitchen, he shifted in his seat and smiled. Hoping that his smile would be the bridge between his cousin's knowledge and her loyalty to him. *I know she was getting ready to tell Mama and Maddie*

171

something about Don and me. Just got that feeling; it was about us.

"Preston? Snap out of it!" Deb giggled and playfully shook her head. "I'll see you later, Cousin. See ya'll! I'll be back over here tomorrow sometime!"

"Alright, girl!" Madisyn yelled.

"I'ma make you some greens and have it ready when you get here tomorrow. Tell Leroy I said hi, and he need to come and see me sometimes."

"I will! You know how my daddy is, Aunt Annie, always sitting in front of the TV. Can't get him away from those westerns, but I'll try to get him to come over with me tomorrow."

"Oh, my goodness. He was into those pictures before he and Ida got married, and he still into those things after she done gone on to glory. My sister spent many-a-days talkin' to me about how that man needed to get away from that TV so much!" Annie laughed.

"Yep, used to get on Mama's nerves!" Deb called into the kitchen.

The goodbyes and banter from the kitchen finally popped Preston out of his trance. "Aye, let me walk you outside."

Deb gleefully laughed once more before making her way to the front door. Preston followed closely behind her. Reaching past, he opened the door and waited for her to go through it. He waited until they were both completely out onto the porch and away from open ears before he spoke a single word or asked any questions. "So, what happened?"

Deb leaned against the rail and slightly frowned at Preston. "When?"

"What you was talking 'bout when you first came in."

"When I first came…? Oh! You talkin' bout when I said something about, he ain't—"

"Yeah, that." Preston folded his arms in an attempt to shield his body from the biting cold that lingered in the air.

"Oh, that was nothing. You know how I am, always running my mouth about something."

Preston looked at the door and then back at Deb. "Come on, Deb. I already know what Don did. So, you ain't gotta try to keep me from it."

Deb lowered her head before reaching in her coat pocket and grabbing her shades. Slipping them on, she nodded her head. "I'm glad you know already."

The chat slowed as Preston's feelings changed from frustration to a strong sense of embarrassment. Deb was known for spilling tea, wine, coffee, you name it. If it was hot, she was willing to spill it, no matter who or what the conversation was about.

"You know, Cuz, I ain't into telling people how to live their lives. Who to love and how to love, but I gotta tell you this. Donald ain't no good."

Preston lowered his head and quickly lifted it back up. "Yo! I got it!"

Preston watched as the neighbors' teenaged sons ran out of their house and into their yard, bouncing a basketball and conversing loudly, as they often did when they came out to play. Two of the other kids who lived two houses down shortly joined them, bringing the usual noise of a typical Saturday afternoon.

"You need to leave him. There's a lot of good guys out there, Preston."

Turning back to Deb, he chuckled. "I'm beginning to believe there is no such thing as a *good guy*."

"Well, there is. You just need to leave Donald alone, and then it'll be easier for you to see. Don't make no sense how he be messing with that man from the grilling station in the cafeteria. Instead of sneaking off in closets and having sex, he need to figure out how to stop burning my chicken tenders when I go up in there. Dry tenders... And then he married too! Don't make no—"

"Wait... hold up!"

Deb leaned her body against the rail.

"What man?!" Preston's mind was all over the place. All he could see was the guy who showed up at his house, defending his wife's honor and ready to beat Donald down for having some sort of affair with her. There was nothing said about him being married to a man! !ho works at the grilling station...in the cafeteria...burning chicken??

"The dude he be messin' round with! You would think that place was some sort of sex dungeon instead of a hospital. Every time I turn around, somebody bangin' somebody. And most of the time, it be somebody else's husband or wife. I don't understand it."

The wind's gush kissed the dried rose bushes that lined the Dixon's yard and hugged the big oak tree that loomed over them. Preston kept his eyes on a few leaves that fell from the tree, onto the grass, and on one of the bushes. "What's his name?" he asked in a low, seething tone.

"They call him Biz, but I think his name is Jeremy or Jerome. It's one of them; I don't really know him like that. I thought you said you knew—?"

"Yeah," Preston said quickly, ending the conversation as he didn't want to add more fire to the flame of Deb's hot tongue. *If she finds out about the other person Donald messing with, it'll for sure be the next tea that's spilled.* "I'll holla at you later, Deb. I need to get ready to get over to the hospital."

"Oh, okay. How is he doing?"

"Still resting, but hopefully, we can get him awake and all soon."

"Yeah, I hope so," Deb said as she fumbled with the contents in her pocket. *Where did I put my bus pass?* She mumbled as she dug around further. Pulling a lump of papers out, she sat down on the edge of one of the rocking chairs and placed the papers in her lap. Preston stuffed his hands in his pockets. His mind was full, causing a throbbing headache.

"Here it go! I gotta get me another bag, keep all this mess in. What about that bitch? What she up to?"

Preston forced his mind back into his now and chuckled. "Still being a bitch," he replied. His mouth balled up into a small circle at the thought of Stephanie crying while being allegedly raped by someone who was supposed to protect her. He looked over at Deb. *I wonder if she knows anything about Stephanie, and… Nah. I'm sure she would've already told Mama. If not Mama, definitely Maddie.*

"Well, we all know that ain't gonna change. And if I catch her around here again, startin' mess, I'm gonna beat her down." Deb stood up and stuffed the papers back into her pocket. "She thinks she got her ass whipped on Thanksgiving; she ain't seen nothing yet."

Preston smirked. "See you later," he said while sitting down on the swing.

"Alright, Cuzzo. Call me if she come back over here, and I ain't here. The Number Ten runs seven days a week now. Straight shot from my house to here."

Preston laughed aloud. "Noted," he said as he leaned back in the chair. He blankly watched Deb as she jogged down the stairs, out into the yard, and down the street to catch the bus. The neighborhood boys were deep into their basketball game. Grabbing one of the decorative pillows that sat neatly on the side of the swing, he put it on his lap and rested his hands on top of it. *They ain't got nothing but fun times and a lit, carefree life*, he whispered to himself as the boys continued with their game, not bothered by anything past what they were up to at the moment. *Stay young, boys, 'cause when you get grown, life has a crazy way of sometimes dealing you bullshit and frustration.* Sighing, he kept his eyes on the boys, hoping that some of their freeness would travel across the street and spread itself into his life.

CHAPTER 16

Boy, why didn't you get that alternator fixed the other day when I told you to?"

Chad waited while his father worked under the hood of his car. "You know how it is, Pop? Stuff happens, and then I just forget."

"Yeah, well, you should never forget about dealing with your car. You need it to go around and look for a J-O-B!"

Chad kept quiet, not wanting to add any extra fuel to his father's budding attitude.

"Have you found anything yet, son? Anything at all?"

"Not yet, Pop. Still looking."

"Well, look harder. You want a life with that gal; you need to be able to support her."

"Yes, sir," Chad answered, hoping that adding "sir" would halt the criticism.

"And me and yo' mama ain't gonna keep paying your bills at that apartment. I know things happen, and sometimes, jobs just get lost, but that's why you always have a backup plan, son."

"Yes, sir," Chad replied again, hoping that his lack of excuses would be enough to quiet his father about his problems with finding adequate work.

"Chad!"

Chad turned towards the sound of his mother's voice and saw that she was standing on the porch. "Yes, ma'am?"

"Come here for a minute."

Happy for the interruption, Chad quickly walked over to his mother. The look on her face told him that something was wrong. "What's the matter, Ma?" He asked while making his way up the steps.

"I think I need to take Ashanti to the hospital. I want you to come with me."

"Okay, but wassup with her? She still got that cold?"

"I think it's something worse than just the average cold. I want to go ahead and take her in."

Chad followed his mother into the house. He shook his head at the clapping coming from the TV. "She love some damn ChiChat," he said under his breath and chuckled at the four women staring back at him and talking to their audience. *A woman's paradise. A show for nobody but women, with women hosts, a packed audience of only women, and always women guests.* Chad walked past the TV, just as the ending theme song of the show was airing. "Well, at least they sistas, got the TV on lock. Badass sistas at that."

"Chad, come on in here and grab a couple of Ashanti's books. We might be down there for a while." Taking one final glance at the women, he lightly bit his lip and smirked before following his mother's orders. Going into her bedroom, he grabbed three books, all with little girls and ponies on them, before flopping down on his parents' bed. Looking down by his feet, he chuckled. "She done bought some more of those ladies' shoes. My mama got it bad for those girls."

"Get the ones with the—"

"Ponies and girls on them! Already got 'em, Ma!" he called out before standing and walking back into the living room.

"She got a fever. I hope it's nothing too serious."

Chad grabbed Ashanti's coat and handed it to his mother. He watched as she placed Ashanti's arms in the coat and laid her on the couch.

"Pick her up for me and bring her to the car."

"How long she been sleep?" He asked while lifting her off the couch and popping the TV off with his free hand.

"All day. You know that ain't like her."

Chad kissed his niece on the cheek as he followed his mother outside and to her SUV. *I guess it's no need to ask about her sorry ass mother. She should be the one taking her baby to the hospital, not Moms.* Using his left hand, he opened the back door and placed Ashanti in her booster seat. Strapping her in, he jogged around to the passenger side and got in.

"I guess I need to tell Pops where I'm going. He already got an attitude about my car." Rolling down the window, he waited a few seconds as his father's head was all the way down and into the car's hood.

"Aye, Pop!" Chad took in a deep breath of the sky's fresh air before calling out.

"That man," Brooke said as she readjusted the heater settings.

"Aye... Pop?!"

Alvin looked up and frowned.

"I'm going with Ma. I'll be back later."

Alvin waved his right hand and proceeded to go back to his task. Brooke pulled the gear to drive and slowly accelerated, stopping next to her husband. "The fever is worse, so I'm taking the baby to the hospital."

"Alright," he said before peeping in the back seat. "Call me as soon as you find out what's going on with her."

"Okay," Brooke replied before driving out of the driveway and onto the road.

Preston watched uncomfortably while the respiratory therapist fiddled with Jordan's respirator. He pressed his body closer to the bed rail while placing his hand on top of Jordan's. "It's warmer," he smiled.

"Yep," the respiratory therapist said.

Preston leaned back in his chair, not realizing he'd said a word aloud. He liked to keep quiet anytime someone was in the room, caring for Jordan. Preston didn't want anything disrupting his care, not even an ounce of conversation from him. He began to feel a bit inadequate at the fact that he didn't know that Jordan's hands would, in fact, be warm. *He is still alive. I act like—*

"His oxygen is good today."

Preston slid to the edge of the chair. "Oh... good."

"Yeah, coming along."

Preston smiled. The therapist wrote a few notes down on her notepad and dropped it into her jacket pocket.

"Can I get you anything? Something to drink?"

"Uh... no, I'm good, thanks, though."

"No problem."

Preston stood up and walked over to the window while the therapist exited the room and into the hall. Looking out at the snow and left with nothing but the occasional beep from one of Jordan's machines and his firestorm of thoughts, he leaned his body against the window and sighed. His mind took on its deed of the powerful picture playing that it always seemed to do when he was left alone with it. *He is Jordan's father... he raped me... he ain't breathing...!* Shaking the movie away, he turned at the sound of the door slowly opening. Stephanie stood in the doorway, with a face full of sorrow and eyes just as puffy as one of Jordan's stuffed animals.

"I thought I'd find you here," she said in a voice just above a whisper.

Preston turned completely towards Stephanie and glanced at Jordan before slowly walking closer to her. "Yeah, had to come and make sure all things are going in a positive direction with him."

Stephanie placed her purse on the bedside table and leaned against the counter. "Well, there is nothing like a father's love."

The conversation fell silent. Two of the hospital's staff swiftly moved past the door while one of the bells on the monitor rang out. Preston's heart jumped into its usual panic mode at the sound of the heart rate's bell alert. Just as fast as it alerted, it had stopped, bringing Preston's own heart rate back to its normal pace.

"Can we talk?"

Preston breathed in deeply. "About what?" He asked as his eyes remained on the monitor. He knew that he couldn't continue to avoid the conversation, and one day, he would have to face it. He knew exactly what Stephanie wanted to talk about, but he asked anyway, just as a time filler. *Any amount of time is better than none, even if it spares me only a few seconds.*

"You know…about what happened at the house."

There it is, she said it. So now, my time is over as Jordan's father. His brain felt like someone had opened his head, drilled deep down through his skull, and dropped hot coals on it. The sting and burn began at the top of his head, eventually making their way down to his face. He felt flushed and needed to sit down. "Did I kill him?" Preston could still hear Janet crying out and hollering that her brother wasn't breathing. *I couldn't have hit him that hard…enough to kill him.*

"Kill? No, mama was just being melodramatic. Ain't nothing wrong with him. Well…maybe just one hell of a sore jaw…I'm sure."

Preston nodded his head in agreement.

"We can go downstairs, grab a coffee or something."

Forcing his way through his anguish, he nodded his head. "Alright," he managed to say before strolling over to Jordan and kissing him on the forehead. He looked at Stephanie and then over to the door as he walked to it and into the hallway, waiting for Stephanie as she kissed and doted on Jordan.

Chad moved the tiny red and green balls on the activity cube that sat on the wall in the children's emergency department. He smiled at Ashanti as she repeated his actions. Around Ashanti's age, two other children sat across from there, playing on another one of the hospital's toys. The phone vibrated once in his pocket, signaling he'd just received a new text message. Moving another one of the toy's balls, he motioned for Ashanti to follow his lead before he reached in his pocket and grabbed his phone.

How is she doing?

Chad leaned back in his chair and typed in a quick reply to Madisyn.

She good… we waitin for them to call her back.

Ok, call me when you get home.

He glanced at Ashanti.

K

Slipping his phone in his pocket, he watched as Ashanti's attention turned from the activity cube to the dragon-looking life-sized cartoon character on the TV. She coughed loudly before sitting down in a small blue chair crafted for children her size.

"It sure is taking them a long time to call Ashanti back."

Chad looked up at his mother before she sat down next to him. "Yep," he agreed. "Maybe we should've waited and taken her to her regular doctor on Monday."

"She doesn't have one," Brooke said before sipping some of her coffee.

Chad shook his head, placed his elbows on his thighs, and put his head in between them. "How she don't have a regular doctor?"

"Your sister, Chile."

Chad and Brooke blankly watched as the dragon danced around on the TV. Ashanti coughed again as she rubbed her eyes and yawned.

"Did Pops call?"

"Yeah, you know he did. He loves that little girl. Just like she was his very own granddaughter."

Chad nodded. "He loves him some Ashanti."

Brooke smiled. "He sure does."

"Was it crowded in the cafeteria?"

"Uh-uh, not too bad. Most of it was closed. All except for the coffee station and the vending machines. All the other areas were closed up." Brooke sipped more of her coffee and smiled at Ashanti.

"I be back. I'ma go down there and get a soda or something."

Brooke nodded. "Get you a bag of chips or something too. You haven't had anything to eat since earlier today. Here it is almost nine o'clock."

Chad stood up and pulled his phone out of his pocket. He rubbed his back pocket and sighed. "That's right, I left my wallet in the car." He looked over at the window and sighed. It was snowing again, something he wasn't too fond of.

"Here, I got some change." Brooke sat her coffee on the table and grabbed her bag off the table.

"It's alright, Ma; I can use my phone." Chad typed in his passcode and opened the web browser to his banking information. He checked both of his checking and savings accounts before closing his phone back and slipping it in his jacket pocket.

"Alright. See you when you get back, son."

Chad peeped over at Ashanti before heading towards the door.

"It was at the Christmas party."

Preston kept his eyes on the two women who laughed and chatted as they worked behind one of the closed cafeteria stations.

"Mama used to have these big Christmas parties after church. Every year on Christmas eve, the family would come over to our house. That's when it would happen."

Preston's interest was now piqued. His eyes moved from the workers to Stephanie. She didn't look like the strong, attitude-filled woman he was used to dealing with. She looked more like a frightened and betrayed person, someone who didn't have a friend in the world and had no one at all to lean on.

"Everyone would be in the living room, dancing and listening to Christmas songs. "This Christmas" by Donnie Hathaway was Mama's favorite. She would dance and sing all over the living room." Stephanie smiled while gazing off in the near distance. "Yep, she loved herself some Donnie Hathaway."

Preston nodded his head and readjusted himself in the chair while fiddling with an empty straw wrapper from Stephanie's straw.

"I was eight when it all started. Uncle James would tell me to go in the kitchen and get stuff. Stuff like… *'Go on and make sure the ice is filled. Or we gettin' low on sodas. Baby, why don't you go and get some more for us old folks?'* "I was just happy that Mama and Daddy were letting me stay up so I would always be willing and ready to help out as much as they wanted me to." Stephanie's smile was now replaced with a slight frown.

Preston leaned closer and placed his hands in front of her, hoping that she would take that as support.

"He would always come in, just as I was bending down to grab more drinks out of the fridge. I don't know, it was like he always knew when my back was turned, and I was in the perfect position for him to..." Stephanie closed her eyes.

"Hey... um... we can talk about—"

Stephanie lifted her right hand but kept her eyes closed.

"At first, it was pats on my butt." Stephanie slid back in her seat, preparing herself to go further. "Then... he would kiss me. On the forehead, at first, before he started kissing me on the lips."

Preston swallowed. The workers laughed aloud, pulling Stephanie out of her trance-like state. She folded her hands before continuing. "A few years had passed since he'd last touched me, so I thought everything was alright. I didn't have to worry about his nasty hands on me. Then one day, he left church early. It rained that day, all day. Told Mama he wasn't feeling good and he was going to go home. He and Aunt Callie went home, but then he told my Aunt Callie that he'd forgotten something at church, and he would be back. Well… he didn't go back to the church that day. He came straight to Mama's house, and that's when he first forced himself on me. I was only thirteen."

Preston shifted in his seat. Although he had more days of not liking Stephanie than he was satisfied with her lately, he hated hearing what had happened to her.

"After he was done, he begged me not to say anything. He promised that if I kept quiet about it, he would never do it again. The pain was so bad. I was scared of what would happen if I didn't do what he told me to do. So… I kept the secret all the way up until…"

Preston's stomach folded into harsh knots. He wasn't quite sure what Stephanie was getting ready to say. Still, he had the strangest feeling that it pertained to Jordan's paternity. His mind left the present moment, visiting the scene of Stephanie's uncle, lying on the floor with Janet screaming and hollering beside him. His mind jumped back to the present, and he gazed at Stephanie. *What happened to him after I left?* Opening his mouth to ask the question, he was silenced by Stephanie as she continued on with her story.

"I got pregnant."

Being that Stephanie's one and only pregnancy, to his knowledge, was Jordan, Preston braced himself for the truth. A truth that he wasn't quite sure on how to morph into *his* truth.

"It was right around the time when we had met at church. Mama… well, she searched and searched until she found the perfect person to help keep the secret."

Preston frowned. "Huh?"

"H-he'd slipped something in my drink… Daddy always told me to never keep a drink out and in the open, unattended. But I was with family, so I figured I could trust my own family. Not really his ass," she frowned. "But Aunt Callie was there, so I thought I was safe. Well… one day, he and Aunt Callie came over to the house when Mama and Daddy was out. I don't remember where they were, but they weren't home. I went to the bathroom, left a glass of iced tea on the living room table, and when I came back, I drank it. The next thing I know, I wake up, on the couch, naked from the waist down with Aunt Callie…." Tears began to form in the corners of Stephanie's eyes. She forcefully wiped her eyes before she continued. "Aunt Callie was standing over me, while Uncle James was standing closer to the door looking all crazy in the face. Aunt Callie was holding a blanket and threw it on top of me. 'Cover up, gal,' she said in a stern, kind of demonic voice."

Preston sighed loudly and shook his head.

"Then he… he told me that if I told anyone what I *think* happened, he'll lie and say that I jumped on him and seduced him. I-I looked over at my aunt, and she said, 'You ain't got no kind of proof, so keep yo' mouth shut.' Aunt Callie had so much hatred in her eyes. She didn't even look like herself. A few seconds later, they walked out of the house together." Stephanie looked at Preston, studying him before she said more. "Six weeks later, I found out I was pregnant."

Preston leaned back in his seat, balled his lips, and lightly bit down on them. Stephanie kept her eyes on Preston, looking for a sign to continue. Preston lowered his head, signaling her to go further.

"I wasn't sure on what exactly happened that day, but when I didn't get my… I took a test; it came out positive. At that point, I knew what the bastard had done because I hadn't been with anyone. From that moment forth, I knew I couldn't trust nobody in the family. I mean, what kind of wife sits back and helps cover up a rape?!"

The women who'd been working behind the station both looked over at Stephanie. Stephanie cleared her throat. The woman turned away from Stephanie and went on to finish their jobs.

"There was two people in the world who I still could count on, though. So, I thought…."

Preston sat up in his chair.

"My mama and my daddy. I was too ashamed to tell my daddy, so… I went to Mama." A tear fell down her right cheek, replacing the makeup stain created by the previous tears. She moved her hands off the table and placed them on her lap. "Mama…she was so nice when she spoke. 'We need to protect our family because family is very important,' she said to me. Poppa was one of the biggest pastors on this side of Baltimore. 'We can't have this out in public, sweetie, tainting your grandfather's name.' So…" Stephanie replanted her hands on the table. "Mama came up with what she called the perfect plan. Get with a nice young man from church, a man who comes from a good family and have some business about himself."

Preston snickered in disbelief and slowly nodded his head. "I guess that's where I came in."

Stephanie nodded. "Yeah. She said you were perfect."

"Sooo… you were already pregnant when we got together?"

Stephanie's silence gave him his answer. He slid out of his seat and stood up, not bothering to say another word before walking off and leaving Stephanie at the table.

CHAPTER 17

Startled out of a deep sleep, Donald hopped up and stood still before trying to gather his thoughts on what the noise could've been that was loudly coming from the living room. The sun had long gone down, causing him to have to strain his eyes to see around the bedroom.

BAM!

Jumping back, his breathing intensified, and his heart pounded so hard in his chest, he thought he was on the verge of having a heart attack. His vision was becoming clearer. *Not again!* Taking advantage of it, he searched the room for a weapon. His eyes focused on the bat, the same bat he'd held the night Ronnie and her husband bombarded him and Preston. He timidly moved his upper body closer to the door while keeping his lower body as still as humanly possible. *Maybe Preston's home.* Another crash interrupted the steady tick of the nightstand's clock. *Nah, that ain't Preston.*

Taking in a huge deep breath, his feelings switched from terror to embarrassment, then pressed on over to shame. Embarrassed that he didn't feel monstrous enough to protect his home and a bit ashamed. Well, ashamed because he was always taught that a man's place was to protect what belonged to him and his family. One of the principles of manhood his uncle taught him before he died. He felt like a failure, failing to do the one thing his uncle took time to teach him. The noise suddenly stopped. He waited a few seconds before moving closer to the door. Starting to the door, he sighed lightly before proceeding to inspect his home. He stepped his right foot out into the hallway with the bat in tow first before lifting his left foot to follow. In an instant, a pair of hands snatched him up. Like he was a mess of debris, flying aimlessly and helplessly in a violent early summer tornado.

"Where the money at?!"

Dazed and confused, Donald squinted his eyes in an attempt to adjust his eyes to another round of darkness. He could see a figure but had no idea who it was.

"If you don't start talkin' right now, I'ma blow your brains out!"

"Put the chair in front of the door! Why you just standing there like some scared lil bitch?!"

Sounds of the couch scraping against the hardwood floor replaced the wickedness of the intruder's voice.

"Listen…my wallet is in the kitchen…on the table... just—"

"That ain't what I want, fool! I should smack yo' stupid ass!"

Donald's mind was in an uproar. He listened hard at the voice but still had no idea who was attacking him. *How the hell did they get in? Why didn't the alarm go off?* Still surrounded by darkness, he looked over at the silhouette of the board he'd just placed over the broken window before he laid down. *The broken window.* His eyes were again beginning to adjust as he peered at the object that was replacing his window. *It's still up, though… How—?*

"I'm not gonna ask you again! Where… is… the…money?!"

"What money?!" Donald yelled. "And who are…?"

"The money you owe! Where it at?"

Donald frowned. Anger was slowly being replaced by the fear and frustration he felt. "I don't have any money," he said in a lighter tone. "All I have—"

"Oh, you got some money. You owe some money!"

"What are you talkin' bout?"

A small whimper escaped from the other side of the room. The man's hard grip held Donald tight, not allowing him to free himself.

"Alright," Donald said. "Let's make sense of this," he said quickly, in an attempt to bargain with him. "I don't have any money, I—"

"Bullshit! Baby! Go in the kitchen and get his wallet."

Great... another Bonnie and Clyde act. Donald listened as the footsteps walked past him and into the kitchen. The person seemed to be much smaller than the person holding him. *Maybe I can rush 'em.*

"I don't see it!"

Donald's eyes were now widened by surprise. "Heather?!"

"What you say something for?! You so stupid!"

"Heather!"

"Shut up! You was supposed to keep yo' mouth shut!"

"I-I'm sorry. I—"

"Shut up before I drop yo' stupid ass!"

Donald sighed a sigh of relief as the assailant threw him onto the couch, finally letting his arm go. He looked at the door and then back towards the intruders. Moving his left foot forward, adrenaline pumped hard within him. He looked back at the intruders again, then moved his right foot.

"Where your card at?!"

The adrenaline rush quickly subsided.

"What ca—?"

"You know what I'm talkin' bout. For the ATM. Your bank card!"

"In my wallet... on the table." A thick flash of remembrance shocked Donald's brain. *You owe money... you owe money... pay me my money...* "Heather... I'll get you what you want."

"Shut up!" The man yelled.

Ignoring him, Donald continued. "You want to be paid for the job, and I understand that. But... I don't have it here. It's at the bank."

"Then let's go to the bank and get it!" The man yelled.

"The banks are closed!" Donald yelled back.

"Yo!" Heavy footsteps came towards Donald, and he sat back further on the couch. "Who the hell you raising your voice at?!"

"Listen, I'm…" Donald sighed and put his head in his hands. "The banks are closed…okay? We have to wait until tomorrow to get it. Now, I give you my word… that I will have the money to you first thing in the morning."

The room fell silent. Donald's eyes were well adjusted to his house and its contents. He still couldn't quite make out who the guy was, but he did see that he was a tall, well-built man.

"What time they open?"

A huge sense of relief grabbed Donald. "Eight-thirty," he blurted out, happy that the man was finally ready to work with him.

"How much?" Not waiting for an answer from Donald, the man turned towards the woman. "How much did he say he would pay you?"

So, it is Heather!

"Um… uh…"

"What you mean… um…uh…?! How much was you supposed to get for shooting the kid?!"

The words stung Donald; his excitement was now at a dangerous level of grief. He'd had that same feeling before when he first heard that it was Jordan who was shot and not Stephanie, his intended target. "I got five thousand!" He said loudly. Twenty-five thousand and some change skimmed his brain. *I ain't about to let these goons take most my life savings…Nope!*

"Yo! I know you got more than five thousand. Living in a house like this and in this neighborhood? Yeah… you can do better than five thousand."

"I swear… that's all I have."

Another round of silence before the guy spoke. "A'ight. Five thousand."

Donald's body relaxed. "I'll get it to you first thing in the morning. Where you want to meet?"

"I can come back over here—"

"No!" Donald hissed. Not realizing just how loud he actually was until the word lingered for a few seconds. "I mean… it would be better for me if we met somewhere. Let's turn on the light so—"

"Nope! The lights stay off. Meet us at Heather's house."

Donald looked towards the kitchen at his stepdaughter. *Heather. Why did it even have to come to this?* "I don't know where she lives."

The man sighed. "Heather, why you ain't tell Pops where you live at?"

"I ain't have no reason to Silk."

Silk? What the hell kind of name is that? Donald remained silent, only having a conversation within himself. *Silk. These young boys today.*

"Look!" Silk squawked.

Donald left his thoughts and focused all his attention on Silk. "Meet me in the parking lot of Dominick's. You know where that is?"

"Yeah, I can do that."

"Alright. You said the bank open at eight-thirty?"

"Yeah, eight-thirty."

"So, I'll be over there at ten. That should give you plenty of time to get it and come over there."

"Okay. Yeah, that's perfect." Donald waited on the couch as Silk and Heather proceeded to the door. *Dominick's? How the hell that hoodlum know anything about a place like Dominick's? I'm sure he can't afford...*

"Silk, you sure you wanna meet at your mama's job?"

Bingo! His mama's job. I knew his ass couldn't have been a customer. Not at Dominick's.

"Shut up! Don't worry 'bout my mama or her job. And you!"

Donald looked up.

"Just make sure you there at ten tomorrow."

"Yeah, I'll be there. Ten o'clock on the dot."

The couple stormed to the front door, opened it, and casually strolled out; as if they hadn't held a man hostage and demanded payment for a deed that was mistakenly done. The front door closed, and Donald fell back and off to the side. He recalled his actions of the last few weeks and sighed loudly. *If I would've just stayed out of it and not hired Heather to kill Stephanie.* He repositioned himself to a more comfortable position. *Crazy thing is… I don't even think Preston was really messing around with her. Now that I think about it. Just a waste of energy.* Closing his eyes, he pursed his lips. "Well, at least my entire savings isn't lost," he said before hopping up and locking the front door, ensuring that the top bolt was tightly locked.

CHAPTER 18

The conversation with Stephanie had his mind spent. Preston leaned his hand against the small counter that sat in front of the cafeteria's salad bar. He observed one of the women who'd been cleaning and preparing to open, drop a wrapped pan of romaine lettuce into its assigned slot before she walked back over to the space where the other woman was working. His eyes remained on the woman, but his mind was with Stephanie and all the drama that she revealed.

"Preston?"

Preston turned.

"Hey, Whatchu doing…? Oh damn, your son. "How's he doing?"

"Chad," Preston smiled. "How's it going?" Hearing Jordan referenced as son now felt oddly strange to him. He didn't like the feeling, but he pressed on anyway. "He's good. Trying to get him off that breathing machine. But anyway, wassup with you? Why are you here? Working here now?"

"Oh, nah. I need to fill out an app to work here, though, but I'm here with my niece. She's up there in the emergency room, can't get her fever to go down."

"Aw man, I'm sorry to hear that."

"Yeah." Chad opened his phone, tapped a button, pressed it against the soda machine. The machine beeped, signaling that it was ready for him to make a selection. "How's Ms. Annie feeling?" He asked while pressing C8. The machine sprang into action to fulfill his paid order.

"She's good. You know Mama; she sure ain't gonna let time in a hospital bed keep her from living."

Chad laughed while retrieving his drink. "Yep," he said while placing his phone into his jacket pocket. "Listen, I'm really sorry about what happened to your son. It's messed up how he got shot … It's just messed up, and I hope that he gets better."

Preston put his head down. "Thanks, man."

"A'ight, I better get back upstairs. Hopefully, they called Ashanti back already. We been here waiting for hours."

"Yeah, they do that. Make people wait a long time. Just to see a doctor and for them to tell you to take some meds, rest, and come back if you get worse."

Chad chuckled. "Exactly!" he said through his laughter. "Like if it wasn't already bad enough that we even came to the hospital."

"Right," Preston nodded. "Aye, I'll walk with you. Give me some time to clear my head." He looked over towards Stephanie before walking away from the emptiness of the closed cafeteria and the emptiness his heart now felt from the draining conversation he had with her.

CHAPTER 19

*Y*ou just had to do it. Heather whispered from within. She sat in the corner of her bedroom, on the floor, while Silk took a small puff of his blunt. *How can he just sit there, like he don't have a worry in the world? I wish I could get away from him.*

"Aye! Go and cook something. I'm hungry."

Heather waited a few seconds before she made any attempt to stand and follow his orders. *I hate him.* Not saying a single word aloud, she stood and quickly walked out of the room and into the kitchen. She knew there was nothing to cook, but she opened the refrigerator anyway, anything to stall another round of beatings. A box of baking soda that was already in the fridge when she'd moved in stared back at her, along with a half carton of eggs and a half-pint of milk. She pulled the eggs out, now remembering that she cooked most of them for Ashanti, and placed the nearly empty carton on the counter. *Please let it be at least two in there.* Opening it, she groaned at the one egg that sat by itself. *Damn.* Looking back towards the bedroom, she sucked her teeth at Silk's loud laugh. *Why is he even here*

213

right now? I wish he'd just go home or go somewhere, like his other baby mama house. Then his ass would stay the night over there and leave me alone so I can finally get some sleep.

"What's taking my food so long?!"

Startled, Heather jumped back. Her heart raced, and her palms were beginning to moisten. *Just close your eyes; it'll be over soon. He wouldn't hit me too long over some food.* "Um, just looking for something else to cook to go with your egg... eggs." *Hopefully, I can stretch this one, make it seem like two.*

"Don't worry 'bout the food. I'ma go handle some business. I'll be back."

Thank you, God. "Okay!" she replied before quickly grabbing the carton and putting it back into the refrigerator. She leaned her back against the counter and watched as Silk walked out of the house. Standing in place, she waited for a bit, just to give Silk some time to make it away from the door. *Thank you, God. Thank you for sparing me another butt whippin'.*

She moved over to the living room, switched the light off, and looked through one of the blinds' broken pieces to see Silk talking with one of the regulars that made claim to her block. Two of the other girls stood talking to each other. As another talked with a man in a silver Cadillac, most likely a potential john. "No, he not!" she gasped when she saw Silk follow the woman behind the old, abandoned gas station. A spot where a lot of the women took their tricks, only reserving motel rooms for their regular clients. "That dirty, nasty bastard! I can't believe he just…."

The ringing of the phone jolted her out of the streets and into her own world. "I bet it's him, lying about something." Making her way to the bedroom, the ringing stopped, just as her eyes landed on the phone. The vibrating started first, then another round of rings. She picked it up and frowned at the sight of her mother's number. "What?!" She yelled at the phone. The phone continued on with its function. Answering it, she looked up at the ceiling. "What?"

"It's your daughter."

"What?"

"Your daughter!" Brooke said louder.

Closing her eyes and slightly shaking her head, she pushed the volume button on the side. "What about her?"

Her mother's voice was louder now.

"Ashanti is sick. We are at the hospital. Just thought maybe you'd like to come down."

"Aren't you over there with her?"

The conversation fell silent. Heather rolled her eyes at the phone. "Hello?"

The picture of her, dressed to the nines and a face full of makeup, replaced her mother's phone number, signaling that Brooke was no longer on the line. "Bitch! Ole bitch hung up on me! What the hell is wrong with that child now? How the hell did she get whatever it is that she got?" Throwing the phone on the bed, she dropped down beside it and closed her eyes. "Dammit!" She huffed before snatching the phone up and pushing her mother's number.

"I'm not in the mood," an irritated Brooke said, not giving Heather a chance at having the first sentence.

"Which hospital y'all at?"

A few seconds passed, bringing on a tittle of frustration on Heather's end.

"Sands Children's Hospital."

"Alright."

"Do you need money for a cab? You shouldn't wait around for a bus this time of the—"

"I got it, and I'll be there when I can." With that being said, Heather clicked the off button.

"Ma, this is Preston, Madisyn's brother."

"Oh, the professor. Hi, nice to meet you," Brooke stood up and shook Preston's hand.

Preston smiled. "Yes, ma'am, it's a pleasure to meet you too."

"They still haven't called her back yet?" Chad asked as he sat down next to his mother and a sleeping Ashanti.

"Nope, not yet."

Brooke kissed Ashanti on the cheek. Preston sat down in a chair across from Chad and Brooke and crossed his left leg over his right.

"I called her mother. She said—"

"Huh? Ma, why?"

Brooke repositioned Ashanti to a more comfortable position on her lap. "Because she should be here with her baby."

"We here with her. That's all that matters."

Preston remained quiet. Jordan entered his mind, followed by Stephanie's story, and then finally, Stephanie's sick and deranged uncle. He passively listened while Chad and his mother chatted about why or why Ashanti's mother shouldn't be there with them while they waited to be seen.

"Chile, she's still this baby's mother. No matter how negligent she is."

"If you wanna call her that," Chad said before he drank a gulp of his drink and sat back further in the chair.

"Hush up, Chadbert," Brooke mumbled.

Preston chuckled. "Yeah, Chadbert."

Brooke laughed and grabbed a Kleenex from the end table and tenderly wiped Ashanti's runny nose.

"Three forty-two!"

Brooke looked over at the door as Chad grabbed the small piece of square paper with Ashanti's visitor number printed on it.

"Finally," Chad said while slipping the paper in his pocket.

Brooke glanced over at Chad before standing. Ashanti repositioned her head on Brooke's right shoulder but kept her eyes closed.

"I guess you'll stay out here with your friend?"

"Yeah, just call me if you need me to come back there."

"Alright, son," Brooke nodded before lifting Ashanti up higher on her shoulder and walking over to the nurse.

"Hi," Brooke said to the nurse before following her through the double doors that led to the exam rooms.

Chad waited until the doors closed before he continued a conversation with Preston. "It's about damn time they called her back. I think we been here for about three hours now."

"Yeah, these emergency rooms take forever to call people to the back."

"Yeah."

The men sat still for a few moments, both looking over at the entrance. They watched as a woman with two small boys walked into the building and signed in at the front counter.

"Uh-uh! Come back over here, Terry!" The woman called out.

Preston smiled at the other child, who was the spitting image of the boy named Terry. "I can't imagine having two Jordans running around."

Chad chuckled and sipped more of his drink. "Yeah, I feel you. I can't even imagine myself with one, let alone two."

Preston nodded his head slowly. He thought of his sister and the fact that she worked as hard as possible to get her life in better order. "Maddie with kids? Uh-uh, naw!" he laughed. "So... you never see yourself with kids?"

"Nope! Something that I ain't tryin' to get my hands all in."

"What about my sister?"

Chad drank the last of his drink and stood up. "She ain't tryin' to go there either." Walking over to the recycling bin, he tossed the empty container in and looked out the door at the snow, lightly falling from the night's sky. *Damn it*, he mumbled at the sight of his sister walking up the sidewalk.

220

Her ass just had to come. He watched as Heather made her way up the ramp and into the grass, making the first set of footprints in the fresh snow. *There's the sidewalk... so lazy.* Chad shook his head as Heather turned back towards the street and away from the hospital. *Good...bye.* He waited until Heather was out of view before he went back to his seat.

"Stupid ass sister."

"What happened?"

"Nah, I was just saying how my stupid ass sister brought her ass up here."

Preston turned towards the door and then over to the other side of the room.

"She left, though. She shouldn't have come over here in the first place."

"Well... I'm sure she wanted to be here for her—"

"Nope! She ain't foolin' nobody. All she wanna do is probably come up here, pretend like she cares about Ashanti so she can get some money or something from my mother."

Preston pursed his lips. "I know all about that," he said as he saw a drug-addicted Leon, suffering from his own bout of financial insecurities. "Yeah, my brother, you know he was like that. Asking my mother for money all the time when he was out in the streets."

"Right. Me, Madisyn, and Deborah saw him the other night."

"Oh yeah? Where y'all see him at?"

"Out in the streets. My car broke down the other night…" Chad stopped himself, remembering the reason why he, Madisyn, and Deborah was out in the car and was able to catch Leon in the act.

"And Deborah? I ain't never heard of her chillin' with you and Maddie… besides when you over at the house."

Chad lowered his head. He thought of the conversation Deborah had with Madisyn, which prompted them to go out that night. *Should I tell him? I know if somebody knew something about me and my relationship, I'd want to be told.*

"Deborah came over to your mother's house…." Chad was quickly interrupted by the memory of Madisyn's disapproval, folding her arms and throwing him a mean ole nasty look.

"Deborah came by the house, and…."

She'll be alright. "Said Leon was on his way to your house."

"My house?" Preston sat up in the chair. "He doesn't come over to my house. Unless it's an emergency. You know he doesn't like Don."

"Right. Something 'bout he had something to tell you."

"Me?"

Chad nodded his head. "Something about Donald and lying and all that stuff."

Preston leaned back and stretched his left leg. *I guess everybody knew Donald was cheatin'. All except for me.* "Oh, okay," he said quickly. Hoping that his response would be enough to end the conversation. *Don't feel like talkin' bout Don and all his shit.*

The entrance door opened, grabbing the men's attention. Chad sat up and squinted his eyes before waving his left hand towards the door. "Oh damn, the bitch came back."

Preston chuckled. "I'm assuming you talkin' bout your sister."

"Man…I can't stand her ass."

"Yeah, but don't call your sister a bitch. You need to be…" Preston frowned. "That's your sister?"

"Unfortunately, yep."

Preston watched as Heather talked with the receptionist. "Yo, she was in my class. Yeah, my class over at TPU."

Chad joined Preston's state of confusion. "Townsend? She barely finished high school. What the hell she doing being in your class?"

Preston's mind went into yet another round of thoughts. She was always so strange acting. He remembered their first encounter; him lending her a book for the class. Then her coming back later and asking about Don… He stood up. *That's Chad's sister? The one who he is always saying negative stuff about. She is his sister? What a coincidence…. Or is it?* He listened as his mind replayed her question about Donald. *How's Donald doing?* Folding his arms, his mind went further as he recounted the day when his complete trust in Donald took a strong, hard left. *Donald murdered my father. Murdered?! Donald murdered...* he heard Heather's voice just as clear now as it was on the day he'd heard them in his classroom a few weeks ago. Preston closed his eyes before Donald's explanation replaced Heather's account of her father's untimely, brutal, and most of all, strange death.

"Yo, Preston?"

Preston opened his eyes and forwarded his attention to Chad.

"You alright, man?"

"Yeah…" Preston responded. His brain was on fire, and his mind was blown. *This is insane!* His mind screamed. Frowning, he looked back at Chad. "Aye, hold up. I thought you said your father was alive and all. He stays home all the time watching the sports station."

"Huh?"

"Your father?"

"Yeah, my pops is still living. Man, whatchu talkin' bout?"

Preston turned from Chad and focused his attention on Heather. She stood next to the receptionist, seeming just as strange as she did the day she told her truth about Donald and her father.

"Preston?"

"Uh… so your father is still alive?"

"Yeah… what are you talkin' bout, man?"

Ignoring Chad, Preston moved closer to Heather, but before he could make it all the way, she was on her way towards him. Her face turned pale as if she'd seen the ghosts of both Tupac and Biggie, coming back to reclaim their legacies.

"Heather?"

"Uh… Um… Profe- Preston."

Chad walked over to Preston. "Look, somebody gonna tell me what the hell is going on?"

"So… Chad is your brother?"

Heather rolled her eyes. "Unfortunately."

"Yeah, my mother gave birth to the devil's spawn before she had me," Chad said before waving his right hand and walking away back over to his seat.

"Whateva," Heather replied before going in the opposite direction.

Preston pivoted his body in Chad's direction first before turning to face Heather. *She seems nervous.* He kept his eyes on her as she flopped down in the chair and placed her hands over her eyes. *How is it that I never knew Chad's sister is...* ignoring his own question, he walked over to Heather and sat down next to her.

"Small world."

Heather removed her hands, revealing tears.

"Hey, you okay?"

"Yeah, I'm fine. I just hate him."

Preston repositioned himself. "Yeah, most sisters and brothers hate each other. That's just how it is sometimes. You know my sister Maddie? Do you know her?"

"No, I don't."

Preston frowned. *Damn, she and Chad really do hate each other. She don't even know Maddie.*

"Well, we call her Maddie, but her name is Madisyn."

Heather shook her head. "No, don't know her."

"Oh, well, sometimes we argue and hate each other too. That's the way it is sometimes."

Heather nodded her head, showing disinterest in Preston's attempt to chat. Preston glanced over at Chad, noticing the look of frustration and rage on his face.

Preston balled his mouth up in a tight circle and released it. Something he's been known to do when he was in desperate need to clear something up or when he was confused. Confusion was the culprit for his actions this time. He looked off into the near distance, thinking of a way to break at least a chip of the ice that held Heather. *How could I be sitting here with this girl who knows Donald, and at the same time, is my little sister's boyfriend's sister?*

"You know, I wish my son had a sibling."

Heather's face immediately turned from a cold tear-stained to a beet red.

Preston flashed a warm smile and went further. Hoping that if he talked about Jordan, then she would chat about Ashanti. *Maybe she ain't as bad as Chad make her out to be.*

"He's alive?"

Preston's heart rate quickened, and his mind was in full force scramble mode. "Yeah, he's alive! Why would you ask me that?"

He's actually alive.

As the tears fell from Heather's eyes, confusion and a hint of fury were in Preston's. He felt something, not quite sure what it was, but he knew the entire situation was strange. Making an attempt to move his chair over to get a better look into Heather's eyes, his mind cleared just enough to better understand that the chairs were connected and didn't separate. Something he'd known, but he didn't have a firm grasp on reality at the moment. A pinch and a burn grabbed the back of his neck, causing the hairs to stand up.

"Heather?"

"Oh God," Heather whimpered.

Preston stood up and stood in front of her. "What is it?"

Heather's face was full of some sort of look. A look that adopted both fear and relief, with an added hint of bizarre.

"Heather?!"

Heather looked up at Preston but didn't utter a single word. Beginning to feel uncomfortable, Preston slowly walked away from Heather and over to Chad.

"Wassup?" Chad asked while nonchalantly flipping through one of Ashanti's books.

"I don't know. I was talking to your sister, and she —"

"What, starting talking to her invisible friend?"

Preston looked at Chad and frowned before sitting down next to him. "Nah, man," he said slowly. It was like she felt a little *too* relieved about Jordan."

"Too relieved? Whachu mean? She don't even know Jordan."

"Right, that's why the whole thing seems so strange." Preston scooted himself back in the seat and looked up at the TV.

"Put it over there." One of the twin brothers said aloud as he moved one of the small blue chairs off to the side.

"No! Stop!" Terry yelled at his brother.

"Travis and Terry, both of ya'll stop," the woman who'd brought them in said in a low voice as she was playing around on her cell phone.

Preston watched the kids as they fought, then played, then fought some more.

"Stop it, Travis!"

"No, you stop!" Terry yelled back.

"Uh-uh! Didn't I tell ya'll to stop?! Come over here and sit down!"

Preston watched as both boys stood up and followed their orders. *Just about Jordan's age*, he mumbled. He looked over at Chad to see that he had his eyes closed. Looking back at the children and then back at the TV, he thought of Heather again and her strange response to Jordan's outcome. *She don't know Jordan, so how...*

Girl, it don't make no sense how they schemed. The twin's mother said to the listener on the other end of her call.

Preston glanced over at the woman and snickered as she pulled a playful Terry back to his seat with one hand and held her phone with the other.

You know how Silk is; he all about the money. Her conversation continued.

Chad opened his eyes to focus on the woman and her quite intriguing conversation.

Preston looked at Chad and then back at the TV. Two little animated girls ran rambunctiously through a field of flowers. A cartoon in which he'd watched his nieces enjoy before.

Yeah, Terry's asthma has been acting up, so we at the emergency room...uh-huh... girl, nah, you know I ain't got insurance right now. Bruce ain't put them on his insurance like the child support people said he was supposed to, and they said I make too much money to get Medicaid, so I gotta bring them here when their asthma act up. Uh-huh... right. Yeah, but back to Silk; his stupid ass done got mixed up with his baby mama and some man she knows.

Chad sat up further in his chair. Confused, Preston leaned back in his. Not sure why Chad was so invested in the woman's conversation.

Yep...wait but let me tell you what I heard... girl, how 'bout his baby mama shot that little boy and made it look like he shot his self... Yeeeessss! Then they got the nerve to be gettin' money from the baby mama stepfather or somebody.

Preston's heart began to race, and his eyes were now just as wide and surprised as Chad's.

"You gotta go to the bathroom, Travis?"

"Yooooo…" Chad said in a hushed whisper.

Travis shook his head no while keeping his eyes glued to the TV.

Uh-huh… that's messed up… and look, I ain't even tell you the real messed up part about all of it.

Both Preston and Chad were on full alert now. Anxious for the woman to go forward.

I don't know how much… but Silk told Sparkle that he would pay her for all the times she hit him up… You know? … Prostitute Sparkle. She said she wasn't gonna keep giving him some… Girl, behind a gas station. Ain't that some nasty mess? But see, Sparkle will do it anywhere… Yeah! But look… Silk been telling her that as soon as his baby mama people pay her for the job, then he would break her off some of it.

"Three forty-three!"

All eyes turned to the teenager with long blonde hair and a man who was no doubt the child's father as she was the spitting image of him. Not bothering to keep watch as the nurse walked the pair through the double doors, Preston's attention was solely on Terry and Travis's guardian.

"Silk," Chad said aloud.

Preston looked over at Chad and frowned.

Chad moved himself to the edge of the chair. "Yo, that's Heather's dude!"

"Heather's—"

"Silk, that's Heather's dude, Ashanti's father."

Lights as bright as the White House's Christmas tree lit up in Preston's mind.

Nah, not Trish, the other one, the mixed one. I think her name is Heather. Yeah… Heather.

Chad's face was as white as the snow that saturated all of Baltimore. At the same time, Preston's was full of confusion at first, followed by anger, and then finally, rage. He stood up and looked over to where he'd had the conversation with Heather just moments prior, and to his dismay, she was gone.

One Year Later…

News Report

Twenty-five years to life is what was handed down today to Heather Hernandez, the woman responsible for the shooting of now, six-year-old Jordan Dixon, in the murder for hire plot. Today marks one year that little Jordan was shot in his grandmother's driveway as his family gathered for Thanksgiving dinner. Police say Hernandez, of Greensway, shot Jordan in a murder for hire plot orchestrated by her stepfather, Donald Kingsly. Hernandez took the stand in her own defense earlier this month and testified that the plot was set against the child's mother and that the child was accidentally shot. In exchange for her testimony, prosecutors agreed to a slightly lighter sentence. Prosecutors say that Kingsly and the intended target have been in a long-time feud over the victim's father. Kingsly's defense team has declined our request for comment at this time. In a separate trial, Kingsly was sentenced to life in prison without the possibility of parole. Alexa Whitely reporting live, Channel Ten Action News. Mark… Tonya… back to you.

Thank you, Alexa. Happily, little Jordan is out of the hospital and at home with his family, Mark said to the evening news audience.

Thank goodness for that. A love triangle that has indeed gone horribly wrong, Tonya followed. *After the break, Meteorologist Josh Cannon lets us know if we'll need the umbrella or the sunglasses for the next few days. Stay with us.*

Preston looked up at the TV to see the meteorologist smiling at the camera before changing the channel to the cartoon station. "A love triangle? Yeah, right." He said as he gathered supplies for Jordan's gastrostomy dressing change.

"Dad, look!"

Preston rubbed Jordan's head. "Yeah, I see him, son." He grabbed the remote controller and turned the TV up a bit louder, making sure Jordan was well into the show before he began removing the tape from his bandage.

Jordan laughed aloud at the cartoon, causing Preston to join him in his own laughter. Saying a silent prayer, he gently tugged at the first layer of tape and stopped before grabbing the fresh roll of medical tape from off the table. He looked at Jordan, and to his satisfaction, glee was still all

236

over his face. Jordan watched his favorite character, Scruff, dance and sing on a commercial displaying himself as a stuffed animal. Thanks to Annie and Madisyn, Jordan already had his own, being sure to squeeze it tight each and every time he caught the commercial on.

"Hey! Hey!" It was heard first before multiple quick knocks on the door, followed by the doorbell ringing.

Preston placed the roll of tape on the coffee table before walking over to the door. Pulling it open, he was greeted by his sister's cell phone, with the news broadcast's video he'd just finished watching. The news community was referring to as breaking news and the trial of the year.

"Twenty! Twenty! And twenty! Oh… and life for the stupid—"

"Yeah, got it!" Preston cut Madisyn off before she went into another rant about Donald and his plan to murder Stephanie. Madisyn moved over to the side to allow Annie to walk in first.

"Hey, Ma."

"Hi, son," Annie said as she hugged Preston before stepping into the house.

Madisyn, close behind, slapped Preston on the arm. "What's going on?"

"Getting ready to change Jordan's bandage."

"Oh, ok, you might wanna take him in the room and do it 'cause Deborah out there with the kids."

Preston opened the storm door and peeped his head out. The cool, crisp dusk air tickled his face while the brisk wind gust massaged it. He saw his nieces first and then Deborah, leaning over in the back seat of her car.

"Hey girls!" he called out.

The girls ran inside and straight over to Jordan.

"Hey! Y'all stop that running in here!" Annie shouted before flopping down in the recliner and reaching over to fiddle with Jordan's hand. "I done told y'all 'bout that running when you in the house."

"Why y'all ain't help Deborah with lil man?"

"You know why, 'cause she out there smoking. I'm still confused about when she even started!" Madisyn said before planting small kisses on Jordan's cheeks. "She just had to get a smoke of her cigarette before she came in."

"I guess all the stress with taking care of the kids by herself since Leon gone and her mama done got tired," Annie shook her head.

Preston laughed. "Well, you could've at least got the baby and brought him in. Dang, Maddie."

"Shoot, that boy heavy, and he ain't walking yet either! Uh-uh, she got it."

"Oh, he'll be walking soon. Just a little behind, that's all," Annie said as she continued to play around with Jordan's hands.

"Yeah, he starting to. He walked a little when Deb brought him to see Leon."

"Did they say when he will be coming out?" Preston sat down next to Jordan and moved his supplies off to the side. "We can do this later."

"K," Jordan replied.

"Hopefully sometime in the next few months. Next week will make six months since he's been clean from that mess. I'm so glad Deborah talked him into going into rehab. He sure needed it."

"Yeah, maybe this time, he won't turn back to it. Now that he's getting professional help," Preston said.

"I'm trusting and believing in God that he'll stay clean this time," Annie responded.

Preston tore off a piece of tape to replace the piece he'd taken off before his family arrived and slowly taped it over the tubing. Jordan hopped down off the couch and joined his cousins, who awaited him.

"Don't ya'll start that running," Annie warned.

"K!" the kids all said in unison before talking amongst themselves and heading off to Jordan's room.

"He tried calling you?"

"Really, Maddie?" Preston frowned and rolled his eyes. "He knows better. I got a block on my phone, so he can't call, even if I wanted him to."

"Well, that's good," Annie responded.

Preston nodded his head at his mother. "I did get a letter from Heather, though."

"Really? When?" Madisyn tilted her head.

"A couple of days ago."

"Why are we just hearing about it?" Annie asked.

"Well, it wasn't really much of nothing. Just her apologizing for hurting Jordan and about how she wishes she'd never agreed to the plan with Don. Oh, and how she was caught up with her boyfriend and his mess. A bunch of excuses and blames."

"Humph, she sees now that some of these dudes ain't worth the time of day," Madisyn chuckled and shook her head. "Now she locked up, and he out living his life. I'm sure he ain't checkin' for her like that. They probably should've locked his butt up too for conspiracy or something."

Preston rubbed his left shoulder. "They tried, but there wasn't enough evidence against him, so they dropped his case."

"I went over to Chad's mom's house the other day, and her daughter is just as cute as she wanna be," Madisyn smiled. "I went over there to braid her hair. Ms. Brooke is a good grandmother, but she don't know nothin' bout doing that baby hair."

Preston laughed aloud while Annie leaned her head back in the recliner.

"I'm glad Ashanti is doing good," Preston said.

"Yeah, they had the court case last week, and the judge granted Ms. Brooke sole custody of her. Her father's mother wanted her, but the judge felt she would be better off with Ms. Brooke and Mr. Alvin."

"Stability," Preston replied.

"Right," Annie added. "Them people got more to offer that baby. Better neighborhood and all."

"Uh-huh," Preston muttered. "Ya'll want something to drink?"

"Yeah, a glass of iced tea would be nice. I should've had Maddie stop to Dominick's to get me some."

"I got tea, Ma," Preston chuckled.

"Yeah, but you ain't got none from Dominick's."

"I can get Stephanie to pick some up for you. You know her counseling sessions are right down the street from Dominick's. You want me to text her for you."

"Yeah, tell her to stop by there and get me a gallon, please."

"Okay."

"How are her sessions going?" Madisyn asked.

"They're coming along. I think she feels better now that her uncle and his wife moved to Texas, and she has now cut ties with her mother."

"Oh good," Madisyn responded. "I'm glad she's doing better. And I'm glad she finally got off you! Wait! I thought her uncle had a heart attack or something."

Preston chuckled. "He recovered and then moved down south somewhere. You do know people can survive heart attacks. Right?" Preston said in a deeply sarcastic tone.

"Boy," Madisyn sucked her teeth. "Shut up."

Preston laughed. "Yeah, I'm proud of Stephanie. She's really getting herself and her life in order. She starts school in the fall and has been focused on applying for scholarships and all. I'm not trying to go there with Steph, and she is no longer tryin' to go there with me. All about raising Jordan and the both of us, being the best parents we can be for him."

Annie smiled, and Madisyn nodded her head while grabbing the remote and began flipping through the stations.

Preston walked into his bedroom and grabbed his phone. Looking over at Donald's side of the bed, he sighed. Although Donald's been in prison for a few months, he still had the hardest time being met with emptiness from Donald's side of the room. His previous space in the closet, without his work scrubs or business suits, and the sound of silence that the midnight hour brought were at its strongest when Jordan wasn't staying over. Shaking away his feeling of loneliness, he tapped Stephanie's number before walking back into the living room to spend time with the people he loved and cherished the most, his family.

Yolanda's Love Note

Hello Loves,

My grandmother used to say, "Baby, if you gotta fight for a man, then he ain't yours in the first place!"
Donald created an entire firestorm that blew up in his face, all in the name of love. Sometimes, it's best to sit back and evaluate a situation. Other times, it's best to walk away. Donald thought he had everything figured out; the ultimate plan to eliminate, in his mind, the competition. In retrospect, there was no competition, just a story Donald made up in his mind due to his jealousy. Because he was jealous and couldn't stand the thought of losing Preston, especially to his ex, he would now spend the rest of his life away from Preston. Not only Preston, but his entire existence as he once knew.

There is nothing stronger than a women's intuition. I believe that we, as human beings, have the power to adopt extra senses when needed. Preston is a man, but he began to feel the power of intuition. Like many of us, he didn't follow when his mind roared that something was different about his man and their relationship. And because he didn't, it brought him heartache and betrayal.
I encourage you, my friend, to never be afraid to remove yourself from unfulfilling and tumultuous relationships, both romantic and platonic. It may hurt when you're in the thick of it, but once you get out, you open the door for better!

Love,

Yolanda

Meet the Author

Yolanda Randolph is the creator of the #Her Intuition Movement, a movement dedicated to empowering and motivating women to be at their best and remind them of their worth. She is the visionary and creator of the podcasts, Her Intuition Movement Podcast and ChiChat Podcast, and the Her Intuition Glow Awards founder. The Her Intuition Glow Awards is an annual show that's dedicated to Domestic Violence Victims and Survivors. The show celebrates women and all the powerful strength that lies inside. Yolanda is also a Credentialed Medical Coder, mother of three teenagers, and the owner of Madisyn, her beloved Yorkshire Terrier.

Yolanda is an avid reader and loves to write as well. She is dedicated to helping young women reach their highest potential through telling her stories. A survivor of domestic violence and many trials throughout her life, she has become persistent with encouraging others; in hopes that she is an inspiration.

Originally from Baltimore, Maryland, Yolanda now lives in Greenville, NC, with her family.

Stay connected with Yolanda
via Social Media:

- *Facebook - Yolanda Randolph publications*
- *Instagram - YolandaRandolphPublications*
- *Twitter – YolandaRWrites*
- *Website – www.yolandarandolph.com*